MURDER IN VERONA

T. A. WILLIAMS

Boldwood

First published in Great Britain in 2024 by Boldwood Books Ltd.

Copyright © T. A. Williams, 2024

Cover Design by JD Design Ltd

Cover Images: Shutterstock

A CIP catalogue record for this book is available from the British Library.

Paperback ISBN 978-1-83518-772-2

Large Print ISBN 978-1-83518-773-9

Hardback ISBN 978-1-83518-771-5

Ebook ISBN 978-1-83518-774-6

Kindle ISBN 978-1-83518-775-3

Audio CD ISBN 978-1-83518-766-1

MP3 CD ISBN 978-1-83518-767-8

Digital audio download ISBN 978-1-83518-770-8

This book is printed on certified sustainable paper. Boldwood Books is dedicated to putting sustainability at the heart of our business. For more information please visit https://www.boldwoodbooks.com/about-us/sustainability/

Boldwood Books Ltd, 23 Bowerdean Street, London, SW6 3TN

www.boldwoodbooks.com

To Mariangela and Christina. With love as always.

1

SATURDAY EARLY EVENING

The bar in the piazza behind the church is the hub of the sleepy little town of Montevolpone. It's here that the locals meet most days to catch up on events, to discuss politics, football and farming – mainly grapes and olives here in Tuscany – and generally set the world to rights. The bar itself isn't large but it has tables outside on the flagstones, protected from the summer sun by parasols, some so faded that the writing on them is barely visible. The master of ceremonies is Tommaso, the affable proprietor, directed by his highly efficient wife, Monica.

Oscar and I received a warm welcome from the two of them and waves and nods of greeting from a dozen customers – predominantly men – who were sitting around enjoying an *aperitivo* as the scorching sun slowly began to head for the horizon. Oscar's tail started wagging as soon as he saw Monica and he made a beeline for her – he knows full well that she holds the keys to the biscuits – while I went around shaking hands before making my announcement.

'Good evening, everybody. I'd like to buy you all a drink because I'm celebrating. Today's my anniversary.'

Tommaso, who knew me well by now, gave me a quizzical look. 'But didn't you get divorced?'

'Yes, indeed, but this is a different kind of anniversary. It's my second anniversary. It was on this day two years ago that I made the decision to move over from England and settle here in Tuscany.' I gave him a broad smile. 'The best decision I've ever made.' I felt a cold, wet nose prod my bare leg and I looked down at my Labrador, a reproachful expression on his hairy, black face. 'All right, Oscar, you're also one of the best decisions I've ever made.' And not the only one – there was of course my girlfriend, Anna, I reminded myself. Since she had entered my life almost a year ago, things had been on an upward trajectory for me.

Tommaso immediately enveloped me in a bear hug before turning towards the others. 'You heard what Dan said: the drinks are on him. Let's hear what you'd like.' He glanced at me first. 'I don't have any Champagne, I'm afraid, but I've got a good spumante from Greve.'

No sooner had he mentioned this than several of the older men started arguing about where the best sparkling wine was to be found. Needless to say, they referenced only Tuscan wines. Italians are immensely proud of their individual regional identities, and when it comes to food and drink, religiously so. As a general rule, I only ever drink Tuscan wines when I'm here, because anything else would be looked upon with mistrust. Besides, to my taste, Chianti is an excellent table wine, particularly when bought in bulk from my neighbour whose family have been winemaking in the Montevolpone hills for five generations.

Partly so as to avoid the evening developing into an acrimonious discussion of the respective merits of different vineyards, and partly because I've never been wildly keen on fizzy wine, I asked for a cold beer and let the others choose whatever it was they felt like drinking. Unsurprisingly here in the Chianti region, most chose to drink red wine.

I joined a group of four locals that I knew well by now. I sat down with them at one of the tables and spent a pleasant half-hour listening to them telling me about all the ways – many of them grossly inaccurate – in which Tuscany is better than England, and then catching up on the local gossip. Maybe it was just because it was the beginning of August and too hot for anything too exciting, but it appeared that this was quite a slow news day and most of the conversation was, inevitably, about the prospects for next month's *vendemmia*, the grape harvest. The bad news, as I already knew, was that the climate had been getting drier and drier over the past few years and the yield had gone down accordingly. I was listening to Old Piero, who with his grizzled, walnut-coloured skin looked a hundred but was probably not even eighty, making dire predictions about the fate of the planet and the serious shortage of olive oil ahead, when our conversation was interrupted by an unusual noise.

It was the throaty roar of a powerful engine coming down the main street towards us at considerable speed. Unlike most car engines, this had a deep, hollow, echoing sound that set the glasses on the table rattling. Oscar looked up from his position in the shade at my feet with an expression of indignation at this interruption to what had probably been dreams of food and squirrels. There was a squeal of tortured rubber on the stone paving slabs as a car came charging into the square and screeched to a halt barely a few inches from a hefty terracotta planter full of lavender in bloom. The engine gave a final snarl and a sinister explosion before a cloud of blue smoke emerged from its exhaust pipes and blessed silence returned. I glanced sideways at my companions, expecting to see outrage at this demonstration of hooligan behaviour, only to see unexpectedly sympathetic expressions on most faces. I turned back and surveyed the car and its driver and immediately realised that this wasn't some teenager in a souped-up Fiat. Far from it.

The car itself was unlike anything I'd seen for a long, long time. I'm not very good at identifying vintage cars but this was a magnificent, cream-coloured, open-topped, old sports car complete with running boards, huge chrome headlamps, wire wheels and, remarkably, no windscreen. But the biggest surprise was the driver. The low door, hinged so it opened forwards, was pushed open and a figure emerged after a considerable struggle. It looked as though the remarkably small driver of this monster had serious mobility issues as getting out of the car took almost a minute. I was on the point of getting up and going over to see if I could help when Giovanni, the postman, laid a cautionary hand on my arm and shook his head. In a low voice, he told me, 'She's a very independent lady. She'll sort herself out.'

At that moment, the driver managed to get to her feet alongside the car and reached up to remove an equally ancient-looking leather flying helmet and goggles, revealing silver hair and sparkling earrings. To my considerable surprise, I found that I was looking at a woman who probably wasn't a lot younger than my mum – and she's eighty-four. I immediately reminded myself that, since turning fifty-seven the previous month, it wouldn't be long before I, too, would find myself in the 'elderly' category. Still, I had to admit that the magnificent car this woman had been driving was a lot different from my VW van or the Toyota Yaris favoured by my mother – and a whole lot more desirable. I turned towards Giovanni – who knows everything there is to know about the residents of Montevolpone and its surrounding area – and shot him an enquiring look. 'Care to fill me in?'

He looked mildly surprised. 'Haven't you seen her before?

Most of us have met her out on the road at some point and some of us are still here to tell the tale.'

'She has a bit of a reputation as a bad driver?'

He shook his head. 'Not bad, just fast. In fact I often see her – or at least hear her – down on the main road burning off boy racers at the traffic lights.'

'Do you know who she is?'

'Yes, she's Violetta Argento. Her son is... sorry, was... Rodolfo Argento, the famous opera singer who died three or four weeks ago. It was absolutely tragic and, as I'm sure you can imagine, Signora Violetta was devastated.'

The name Rodolfo Argento sounded vaguely familiar, but I'm not an opera buff. Anna loves opera and I felt sure she would have recognised the singer's name immediately. 'How awful for the whole family. I'm very sorry to hear that. What about Violetta? Does she live locally?'

'I'm surprised you haven't seen her – or at least the car – as she doesn't live that far from you.'

I had bought myself a little house in the hills just south of the village the previous year and often walked the paths and tracks around it with my four-legged friend. I'd been getting increasingly familiar with all the little houses and farms dotted over the landscape and I could hardly believe how I could have overlooked such an unusual pairing – the ancient car and its similar-aged driver.

'How strange. I know I would have remembered a magnificent old car like this. Where does she live?'

'Villa Diana. Just over the hill from you.'

I immediately knew where he was talking about. 'I always thought that place was uninhabited. Oscar and I sometimes walk past it and it looks permanently locked up.'

'No, she lives there, all right – just her and her housekeeper.'

The villa was barely a couple of kilometres from my house, set on top of a little hill, surrounded by a high brick wall and a dense plantation of trees, mostly cypress and umbrella pines. 'But surely she needs to drive past my house to get to the villa, doesn't she?'

Giovanni shook his head. 'No, she uses the lane on the other side, from the direction of Empoli. It's far less rough. That's the way I go when I have mail for her. That's probably why you haven't noticed the car before. The Bugatti's ninety years old and it doesn't like potholes.'

'A Bugatti, wow. I bet something like that cost her a packet.'

'She told me it was a present from her brother. Apart from opera, he was crazy about cars and she obviously feels the same way about them.'

I nodded approvingly. 'Generous brother. The most I've ever got from my brother is a bottle of Scotch at Christmas. What about maintenance? Is there a Bugatti garage around here?'

'I expect so – after all, they're still making cars – but she's surprisingly handy when it comes to car mechanics. She doesn't do any of the heavy stuff any more, but I often see her with her head under the bonnet of that thing.'

I was impressed and made a mental note to update my views on elderly ladies.

Signora Argento retrieved a walking stick from the car and came over to the café, walking with some difficulty. As she did so, Monica appeared from inside and greeted her with a smile.

'Signora Violetta, lovely to see you. Your usual?'

Violetta Argento smiled back and nodded before taking a seat at the table alongside ours. Oscar, always pleased to meet a member of the opposite sex, pulled himself to his feet and wandered over to say hello. He was greeted with a warm smile as she immediately made a fuss of him. While she did so, I took a closer look at her. She was quite tiny, but she still had a commanding presence and her eyes were bright, although the dark rings below them indicated the depth of her grief for the death of her son. After greeting my dog, she looked across at Giovanni and said hello to him. He was quick to introduce me in return.

'Good evening, Signora Violetta, have you met my good friend Dan Armstrong? He's English.'

'Good evening, Signor Armstrong.' She smiled graciously and I felt almost as if I were in the presence of Her Majesty Queen Elizabeth. 'Are you here on holiday?'

After a couple of years here, I'm getting quite good at identifying Italian accents and I could immediately tell that she wasn't originally from Tuscany. At a rough guess, I would have said she was from somewhere further north – but not from as far north as me. I gave her a smile in return. 'Good evening, Signora, I'm pleased to say that I live here now, in fact not that far from you.' I went on to explain exactly where my little house was and it was clear that she recognised it from my description.

'And what is it you do, Signor Armstrong? You look far too young to have retired.'

I took considerable heart from this observation although, in fairness, she was probably at least twenty years older than me so, inevitably, I was bound to look young in her eyes.

'I used to be in the police force in London and now I have my own investigation agency here in Florence.' I saw an immediate glint of interest in her eyes and was quick to debunk any notions she might have had of me as another Philip Marlowe. 'It's mostly boring stuff like missing persons or, I'm afraid, marital infidelity.'

A sour expression appeared on her face. 'I can well believe it in this day and age. Whatever happened to people's moral compass?'

Fortunately, I was saved from any further discussion of this thorny subject by the arrival of Monica with Signora Violetta's 'usual' drink. To my further surprise, I saw that this was a glass of beer, just like the one I was drinking. Somehow, I'd been expecting either lemon tea or at most a glass of sherry – although the Italians don't go in for sherry the same way my parents and their friends still do.

After Monica had gone off, Signora Violetta returned her attention to me. 'A private detective, you say? How fascinating, and how useful.' For a moment, it looked as though she was going to say more, but then she sat back and sipped her drink.

I said nothing and gave her time but at that moment my phone started ringing and I saw that it was Anna. She had moved in with me two months ago to see how we got on together and things were going really well between us in spite of a few wobbles caused by the constraints of my job, which sometimes took me away from her. I'd been doing my very best to concentrate as much of my attention as possible on her rather than on my work, in the hope of avoiding our relationship ending up like my ill-fated marriage.

I answered the call. '*Ciao, bella.*'

'*Ciao*, Dan, I imagine you and Oscar are at the bar, right?'

'You know me so well, *carissima*.' Our normal language together is English, which she speaks almost perfectly after having lived and worked in the UK and having formerly been married to an Englishman for twenty years or so. 'Where are you?'

'I'm still in Florence and I'm calling to ask if you feel like coming into Florence and staying at my place tonight. Virgilio and Lina have invited us for a meal.'

This sounded good although I knew that it would be even hotter down in the city. She was still hanging onto her apartment and, luckily, it's in a five-hundred-year-old building whose thick stone walls do a pretty good job of keeping the temperature acceptable.

'Sounds good to me. Give me half an hour to walk back up and collect the car and I'll be with you by seven-thirty or so. Is that okay?'

'Perfect. I'll call Lina back and say yes.'

After putting down the phone, I picked up my beer and drained it, my mind on the elderly lady alongside me. Had I imagined it or had she been about to consult me about something? I glanced at my watch again and realised, regretfully, that this would have to wait, or I would be late for my dinner date in Florence.

2

SATURDAY EVENING

I got to Florence in good time and left my van in the courtyard of
the Renaissance building in the *centro storico* where I had my
office. From there, it took me twenty-five minutes to walk to Anna's
apartment just on the other side of the Ponte Vecchio but I knew
from experience that I would have struggled to find a parking
space any nearer. On a cold January day, it would have been no
more than a fifteen-minute walk, but now, in midsummer and at
the height of the tourist season, the city was absolutely packed. It
took me an age to navigate my way through all the sightseers,
making sure that Oscar didn't stick his cold, wet nose where he
shouldn't. Nevertheless, as usual, even the oppressive crowds
weren't able to extinguish my love for this wonderful city. Every
time I walk around the centre, I make a point of looking out for
new discoveries – whether a particularly beautiful fresco painted
high up on a Renaissance façade, or something as simple as an
iron ring in a wall where horses would once have been tethered.
Yes, Florence just exudes history.

Anna knows all about Florentine history. She's a lecturer in
Medieval and Renaissance History at Florence University and over

the past few weeks, she had been spending quite a lot of time in the university library, researching a paper she was writing on Cosimo il Vecchio, the founder of the Medici dynasty. Being with her had considerably broadened my cultural and historical knowledge, although there was so much history here in Tuscany that I knew I had no chance of ever reaching her giddy heights.

I found her wearing a light summer dress and looking gorgeous. Oscar evidently agreed as he trotted across to stand up on his hind legs against her, tail wagging furiously. She scratched his ears then shooed him off, caught hold of my arm and led me straight back out again to meet up with Virgilio and Lina.

Virgilio Pisano is my best friend here in Tuscany and we have a lot in common. I used to be a detective chief inspector at Scotland Yard, and he still works as an inspector in the Florence murder squad. He and I play tennis together and I sometimes help him out when he has a case involving English speakers. In return, he often puts business my way. His wife, Lina, started working for me as my PA in April this year and has taken a load of work off my shoulders as Dan Armstrong, Private Investigations has begun to gather pace. Tonight, Anna informed me, we were meeting them at a new pizzeria that had only recently opened. This was on the south bank of the River Arno, a fifteen-minute walk from Anna's apartment, and there were tables outside in a little square close to the remnants of the old city walls.

Virgilio and I had an agreement that we would do our best not to talk shop when in the company of our partners. Even so, I could see that he was bursting to tell me something. Luckily, both Lina and Anna know the two of us so well by now that Lina took it upon herself to tell him to, 'Just spit it out and get it over with so that we can get on with our meal in peace'. Virgilio gave her a grateful smile and broke the news to us.

'My big news is that my promotion from inspector to *commis-*

sario has just come through, so that makes you and me the same rank, Dan.'

I clapped him on the back and Anna gave him a hug before turning her attention to his wife. 'How do you feel about this, Lina?' I knew that Lina, like Anna, had been feeling a bit left out from time to time as work had intervened in our relationships. I'd been worried that Virgilio's work had been overlapping and impinging on his private life and I was delighted to see Lina smile in return.

'According to Virgilio, this means he'll probably be spending more time in the office and so, hopefully, he might have a more normal schedule, instead of being called out at all hours.'

Virgilio and I exchanged glances. Neither of us said anything, but I knew from personal experience that more responsibility doesn't necessarily make for more leisure. Time would tell, but for now, we celebrated. After we'd drunk a toast to him, I changed the subject and mentioned my brief meeting with the mother of a famous opera singer. As I'd expected, Anna knew all about him and so did Virgilio – although in his case, in a non-music-related way.

Anna was the first to respond. 'Rodolfo Argento died last month and he was a real colossus in the opera world. He was a child prodigy and he was already playing lead parts when still in his early twenties. His death at, I think, forty or so was a tragedy. I can only imagine how his mother must be feeling.'

I nodded in agreement. I knew how I would feel if anything were to happen to Tricia, my daughter. After a long sigh, Anna picked up the conversation again. 'Rodolfo Argento was a larger-than-life character both onstage and off it. He was a fearless rock climber, he skied like an Olympian, but the love of his life was motor racing. He was ever so handsome and his legions of – mainly female – fans must be distraught at his untimely death.

Above all, he had a wonderful voice and people have compared him to the most famous of Italian tenors like Caruso or Pavarotti.'

Lina joined in. 'I'm not so sure that cars were as important to him as women. He had quite a reputation as a womaniser. The gossip magazines were always full of photos of him with his latest conquests. How did he die, Anna? Not natural causes, I imagine.'

'I'm pretty sure it was a car accident. Ironic, really, considering his lifelong love of motor racing.'

Virgilio took over from her. 'He was going too fast and his car crashed into a tree on a twisty road in the hills above Lake Garda.' He lowered his voice. 'But I remember hearing that a nearby witness said he just drove straight into the tree at speed without braking so, to my mind, it was more probably suicide, but it was all hushed up.'

I couldn't help asking a technical detective question. 'Could he have had a problem with his brakes?' I almost added, *or might somebody have tampered with them?* but I restrained myself. This was supposed to be a pleasant night out with two close friends, not an opportunity to talk shop. As I bit my tongue, it occurred to me that maybe the opera singer's mother might have been entertaining similar thoughts. If so, I told myself, surely she would speak to the police rather than to a random private eye she had happened to meet at the bar.

Virgilio's answer was far from conclusive but, once again, I stopped myself in time. This was a social evening, not work. 'From what I've heard, the Verona police checked the wreckage of the car, but the vehicle was so badly damaged, it was impossible to be sure. At the moment, the most likely explanation is that for some reason, he just decided to end it all, although it was put down to misadventure.'

Anna shook her head sadly. 'Dan and I are going to a concert in Verona next Saturday. I wonder if there'll be any sort of commemoration of his death?'

Virgilio – who knows me very well by now – shot me a sceptical glance. 'I didn't know you were an opera buff, Dan. Is this something new for you?'

I grinned back. 'I'm an opera virgin, Virgilio. The tickets were a present to us from Anna's daughter, Virginia. I'm going with an open mind.' I could have added *and some ear plugs* but I restrained myself. Anna and I have very different tastes in music and I was keen to demonstrate that I was a modern Renaissance man and open to all new experiences – within limits. Anna smiled at me and put her hand on my arm.

'And I'm sure you'll love it, especially in the Arena.'

Lina shot us an envious look. 'How wonderful! I've always wanted to go to a concert in Verona's Arena. Imagine sitting in a real Roman amphitheatre that's even older than the Colosseum in Rome. The sense of history must be amazing, let alone the music. What are you going to see?'

'*La Traviata.* It's one of the classics and the perfect introduction to opera for my philistine boyfriend. He doesn't know what he's been missing.' Anna grinned and glanced across at me. 'By the way, Dan, have you booked us somewhere to stay yet?'

'I'm still trying, but I'm struggling to find one that'll let us bring Oscar. Besides, even if I find one, there's the problem of what to do with him while we go to the opera.'

Lina was quick to offer to look after Oscar. This was very kind, but I was trying not to take advantage of her, particularly as she was now working for me. I thanked her and told her I'd keep trying before bothering her. In fact, I knew that she loved having him, but he was always returned to me a couple of kilos heavier than before, as she was still a sucker for his *I'm starving* look.

Any further talk was interrupted by the arrival of our pizzas.

These were enormous, overflowing from the already larger than average plates, and they tasted as good as they looked. We had all opted for the same thing, the house seafood special, and the generous mix of prawns, clams and mussels was mouth-watering. We drank cold white wine from southern Tuscany and it was a very pleasant evening all round.

But I still couldn't stop thinking about the dead opera singer, his badly damaged car and his elderly mother who might or might not have suspicions about his death. That's the trouble about being a detective – there's no on/off switch in the brain.

And my divorce was the living proof of that.

Anna and I both managed to sleep reasonably well that night in spite of the heat but we agreed next morning that we would head back into the country for the rest of August while the temperature in the city remained in the mid- to high thirties. She had work to finish so she agreed to drive out to join me later that afternoon, but I set off early on Sunday morning and the first thing I did when I got back to my place was to slip back into shorts and trainers and take Oscar for a good long walk before it got too hot. Black dogs – not to mention Englishmen – and hot sunshine don't mix. Out of curiosity, I decided to walk up through the olive groves to take a better look at the villa belonging to Violetta Argento. In the shade of the olive trees, the temperature was still acceptable, but I knew that by lunchtime, it would be far too hot for anything too strenuous – for Oscar or for me.

When we reached the top of the small hill, I walked past the firmly sealed four-metre-high iron gates I had seen before but then turned off the track and carried on all the way around the high brick walls for a change, until we reached the far side of the estate. Here I discovered a second entrance, this time with the gates wide open, facing the gravel lane described by Giovanni the postman. Oscar and I stopped there for a minute, enjoying the shade cast by the trees surrounding the villa and admiring the building that was just visible through the branches. It was a classic Tuscan villa, not enormous, but certainly with space for several big families to live here. The walls were a traditional light-ochre colour, bleached even lighter over the years by the sun, and the windows were protected by dusty, dark-green louvred shutters. It looked old and I felt pretty sure that it had been here for centuries. There wasn't a breath of wind and it was good to rest for a couple of minutes before heading back out into the bright sunlight again.

I was just thinking about setting off when I heard a sound that I immediately recognised. This was coming from one side of the building, first muffled and then louder. There was the crunch of gravel and Violetta Argento hove into view at the wheel of her beloved Bugatti. I caught hold of Oscar's collar and stepped out of the way to let her past, but I was surprised to find that she stopped and switched off the engine. Once again, this was achieved with a loud bang followed by a flash of flame and a cloud of smoke from the exhaust that made both Oscar and me jump. The driver extended a leather-clad hand towards me.

'Good morning. You're the English detective, aren't you?' She was wearing her leather flying helmet and goggles but otherwise she was very elegantly dressed. 'I recognised your lovely dog. I was going to come and visit you one of these days. I'm just on my way to church now but I wonder if you could spare me a few minutes later. I'd like to talk to you about something.'

My ears pricked up. I had a shrewd idea what this 'something' might be but I made no comment, waiting to hear what she said. But all I got for now was an invitation.

'If you don't have plans, could I persuade you to come and

have lunch with me today? Do, please, bring your lovely Labrador.'

Whether it was just because he realised he was the subject of the conversation or whether he had picked up that Signora Argento had issued an invitation to lunch, Oscar started wagging his tail. Taking my lead from him, I thanked her for the kind invitation and we agreed that I would drive back here at noon. She gave me a cheery wave, started the car again and roared off, wheels spinning, in a cloud of smoke and dust. As I picked pine needles and dust out of my hair, I looked down at Oscar, who was sneezing.

'And you'll need to be on your best behaviour. If you try jumping up at her, you'll knock her over.'

He looked mildly offended. Of course he would be on his best behaviour – she had invited us for lunch, after all.

3

SUNDAY MIDDAY

At noon on the dot, I drove up to the villa and parked my van alongside the Bugatti, noting that this was almost a metre longer than my vehicle. Close up, it was a gorgeous piece of nineteen-thirties engineering and the shiny, red, leather seats could no doubt tell many tales of the rich and famous – or infamous. After admiring it and marvelling at how remarkable it was to see something like this still in everyday use, I repeated my instructions about being on his best behaviour to Oscar and together we walked over to the front door. There was a brass knocker almost the size of a lifebelt on the door and a handle on the wall alongside it. I opted to give this a tug and heard a bell echoing around the interior as a result. Twenty seconds later, the door was opened by a grey-haired woman, probably in her seventies, dressed from head to toe in black. She gave me a respectful nod of the head and beckoned to me to enter.

'If you would like to follow me, Signora Violetta is waiting for you in the small lounge.' Her accent told me that, unlike her mistress, she was from around here.

It came as no surprise to hear that there was a choice of

lounges in a place like this. Even the entrance hall was bigger than my living room. We walked down a marble-paved corridor to a charming room looking out onto the rear garden. The room contained a grand piano but still had space to spare for half a dozen bulky armchairs. An unexpectedly modern hi-fi was playing opera music – thankfully not at full volume – and I had a sneaky suspicion that the male singer's voice would prove to belong to the recently deceased Rodolfo Argento. The garden itself was a delight and clearly had involved a lot of work, not to mention an enormous amount of water to irrigate it – and water is expensive. This, as much as the historic house and the classic car, convinced me that Violetta Argento was in a very different income bracket from my own.

My hostess was standing by a wide-open pair of French windows, staring out into the garden. The housekeeper stopped at the door and coughed politely. 'Your guest has arrived, Signora Violetta.'

Violetta turned towards me and smiled as she saw Oscar. His tail started wagging in return as she waved us forward and the housekeeper retired silently.

'Thank you, Teresa. And thank you for coming, Signor Armstrong. I hope I haven't disturbed you too much on a Sunday.'

I assured her that she hadn't interrupted my plans and she pointed out through the French windows. 'Shall we sit outside? It's pleasantly cool in the shade.'

I followed her out to the terrace and we sat down at a beauti-fully ornate, marble-topped table with wrought-iron legs. Although it was still far from cold out here, there was definitely a more pleasant temperature than in the direct sunlight. From the position of the sun, it was clear that this side of the house faced north-east and we were sheltered from the midday sun not only by the bulk of the villa but by the protective screen of trees that surrounded it. Seen close up, some of these looked almost as old as the house and I commented on the fact. Violetta nodded and gave me a quick history lesson.

'The villa was built between 1515 and 1516 and has been owned by just three families since then. I belong to the third generation of the Argento family to have lived here. Many of the trees were planted several centuries ago.'

At that moment, the housekeeper reappeared with a tray. On it were two bottles of Beck's beer and a little plate of salted biscuits. Violetta gave me a little smile. 'I do like a cold beer on a hot day. I seem to remember seeing you with a beer in front of you as well. Is this all right?'

I nodded gratefully. 'Absolutely perfect, thank you.'

She picked up a generous handful of biscuits and indicated Oscar, who had adopted his 'faithful but starving hound' look. She shot me an interrogative glance and I nodded in response. She held out her palm and he very delicately retrieved the biscuits with his tongue and lips and swallowed them in a split second. She wiped her hand on an immaculate linen napkin before reaching for her glass and holding it up towards me.

'Your health, Signor Armstrong.'

I clinked my glass gently against hers. 'And yours, Signora Argento. Thank you for the invitation.' I thought about asking why I'd been invited but decided to leave it to her to make the first move. As it turned out, I didn't have long to wait.

She shot me what my gran would have described as a canny look. 'And now you'd probably like to know why I asked you to come here – and it wasn't just for the company of a tall Englishman and his lovely dog.'

'I must admit to being a bit curious.' And I was. I caught her eye and took a chance. 'Might it have something to do with your son by any chance?'

Just for a moment, I glimpsed the grieving mother beneath the businesslike exterior. Losing a child has to be an awful experience and I gave her a few moments to recover and regain her decisive persona. Finally, after wiping her eyes with the napkin, she continued. 'Rodolfo is indeed the reason I wanted to speak to you.' Her voice was hoarse but under control. She set down her glass and looked me square in the eye. 'You see, I believe he was murdered.'

So my hunch had been confirmed. I decided to press her a bit more just to be sure. 'So not an accident, a mechanical fault or suicide?'

She gave a dismissive snort. 'An accident? Impossible. He was a better driver than I am, and I haven't had a single accident in sixty years at the wheel. As for mechanical failure, he lavished more care and attention on his cars than on any of his ever-changing panoply of women, and he loved his E-type most of all. It used to belong to my brother, Carlo, who died seven years ago now. It might have been old, but it was in perfect working order.'

'That's the vehicle he was driving at the time of the crash: a Jaguar?'

'Yes, his beloved pussycat; that's what he called her. As for suicide, that's quite out of the question. He phoned me only the day before the crash and was boasting that he'd just been invited to perform at La Fenice in Venice at Christmas in front of half the crowned heads of Europe. He was justifiably very proud and looking forward to it immensely.' She reached for her glass again and took a soothing sip. 'There's no way he would have wanted to take his own life. None whatsoever.'

I was impressed, not just by her evident conviction, but also by her lucidity and fluency. Before coming here this lunchtime, I had checked her out on the Internet and had discovered that she was eighty-one years old and clearly as sharp as a tack. I picked up my own glass and sipped some of the refreshing, cold beer while I reflected on what I'd just been told. Of course, this chimed with what I'd been wondering since the previous night. The question was to what extent the murder hypothesis was credible. I did a little bit of digging.

'If we rule out accident or suicide, that leaves us with foul play. Can you think of anybody who might have wanted your son dead? You mentioned his women friends; was he in acrimonious relations with any of them? What about money? Did anybody stand to gain from his death? Then there's professional jealousy – did any of his rivals envy him enough to want to do away with him?' I gave her a little smile to soften my words. 'I'm sorry to ask difficult questions but that's what I've been trained to do.'

I was relieved to see her smile back at me. 'I quite understand. Feel free to ask whatever questions you like, but can I ask you something first: can I take it that you're prepared to look into this for me? You would have to take a trip to Verona, which is where he lived... and died.' Her voice faltered for a moment but she rallied. 'I have every intention of paying you for your time and reimbursing whatever expenses you have. After all, Verona is several hundred kilometres away.'

I had come prepared and I handed her one of my sheets detailing my rates. She pulled out a pair of reading glasses from her little handbag, perched them on her nose and scanned quickly through it before looking up and nodding. 'This all seems perfectly acceptable, Mr Armstrong. When can you start?'

'How would the middle of the week sound?' It occurred to me that I could maybe combine it with my visit to the opera. As she had said, Verona was a fair distance away.

She looked pleased. 'This week would be wonderful. Now, let me try and answer your initial questions. Please repeat them for me.'

'Can you think of anybody who might have wanted your son dead?'

She replied without hesitation. 'His wife, of course.'

This came as a surprise. From what Anna and Lina – and, indeed, his mother – had said about him, I had had him pegged as a single man with a taste for the ladies. What, I wondered, had his wife thought about that?

'I thought you said he had an array of different women in his life?'

'Yes, but he finally took the plunge and got married to Alessia last year.'

'When exactly?'

'Last September. But the fact is that she spent hardly any of the three months before his death with Rodolfo. I wouldn't be surprised if she didn't have another beau.'

'When you say *another*, are you implying that she might have had a number of lovers?'

There was steel in her voice when she replied. 'I'm not *implying* anything, I'm *telling* you. There's just something about her. She's far too good-looking for her own good. I'm sure she must have had other men.'

Considering her son's reputation, and what she had just said about the stream of women in his life, this seemed a bit malicious, but I didn't press Violetta any more for now. My Internet research this morning had also included a quick look into her son's background and this had confirmed his reputation as an inveterate womaniser. If my thirty years at Scotland Yard had taught me anything, it was that rejection, jealousy and bitterness can be powerful motivators for murder. I pressed on with my questions.

'What about life insurance? Did his wife stand to do well out of his death?'

To my surprise, I spotted an expression of what could have

been contrition on Violetta's face. 'He had none. That's my fault. I handled all his business affairs and I was in the process of hunting around for a better life insurance deal when his old policy came up for renewal. If I'd been a bit quicker, things might be different, although there's no lack of money in this family.'

I had already worked that out, but I made no comment. 'If he had been insured, you would have insurance investigators crawling all over the place. So in this case, there would have been no benefit to his wife to see him dead. Maybe that simplifies things. Going back to your son, do I assume that there were lots of unhappy partners strewing his past?'

She nodded. 'I'm afraid so.' She paused and I saw her take a deep breath. 'I'd better tell you myself, before you hear this from anybody else – and you will. Rodolfo was a brilliant singer and a wonderful son, but he had an awful reputation with women. He could be generous and loving but he was pathologically incapable of keeping his hands off other women and, because of his looks and his fame, there were any number of them only too happy to be handled.' A frustrated note entered her voice. 'I spoke to him numerous times about this, but he never changed his ways.'

'So might one of these women have harboured such resentment against him that she decided to murder him?'

'Anything's possible, although why now? After all, he'd been with Alessia for well over a year and married for almost ten months before his death. Why should a resentful woman wait so long? No, I have no doubt that the murderer was Alessia – either directly or by proxy.'

'But if *she* was the one having the affairs, why was *he* murdered?'

She gave me the sort of expression that Oscar gives me when I ask him if he wants a biscuit. 'Money, of course. What else?'

'That was going to be my next question. Did he leave a will and what were its provisions? Did she inherit everything?'

She shook her head. 'If I hadn't stepped in, she probably would have done. Rodolfo had a pathetic trust in people even though time and time again, this trust was betrayed. When he told me he was getting married, I insisted he prepare a new will. Unfortunately, there was no way to alter the fact that in the event of his death, Alessia would inherit half his estate – that's the law in this country, more's the pity.' There was a tougher note in her voice now and my conviction that she was a very determined woman was reinforced. I wondered how this interference had gone down with her son. After all, according to what I had read on the Internet, he had been almost forty, so I would have expected him to look after his own personal finances rather than leaving these to his mother. What sort of relationship had they had? But, for now, I didn't ask.

'So how was his estate divided? If his wife got half his estate, who got the rest of his money? For that matter, I'm assuming he was a wealthy man, but I could be wrong. Did he leave a lot?'

'He was indeed a rich man. We are fortunate to be a wealthy family, but, in the course of his amazingly successful singing career, he built up a considerable fortune of his own.' She gave me a wry smile. 'Which is just as well, considering how much he spent on his women and his hobbies. As far as the conditions of the will are concerned, Alessia, as I said, received a very healthy sum. His agent received a million euros – although that struck me as a ridiculously generous amount – while the remainder of his estate came to me.' From the way she used the word 'million', I had the impression she considered this to be a trifling amount. In that case, his widow must have received an eye-watering sum, and I knew all too well that the attraction of even a million euros would be more than enough to create a compelling motive for murder for many people.

'You mentioned a business. Could you give me some detail of that?'

'The Argento family business is a large company involved with the import and export of agricultural products and machinery. It was founded by my great-grandfather in the nineteenth century and it's gradually grown to its current size and importance. Although Rodolfo had a one-third share, the business is run by my brother's children.' She paused and gave me a decidedly smug look. 'But I take an interest in all major decisions.'

I couldn't help thinking that having to run everything past an eighty-one-year-old for approval couldn't have made for easy running of the company for her brother's children. There was something odd here.

'How is it that you have an interest even though they run the business?'

'Because I represent Rodolfo. When our father died, he left two thirds of the shares in the company to my brother for his children and a third to Rodolfo. It never occurred to my father to include me, even though I'd been working there, effectively helping him run things, for twenty years. When my brother died seven years ago, his children inherited one-third share each. This of course has ensured that my brother's two children have jobs for life.' A sour note entered her voice. 'Unfortunately, Alfredo, his firstborn, is far more suited to a life of luxury and idleness than to running a company, so for Rodolfo's sake I've always kept an eye on things ever since.'

'Rodolfo himself took no interest in the business?'

She shook her head. 'He wasn't interested in commerce. He was following a far more noble vocation.'

I thought that a bit presumptuous but I made no comment. Instead, I asked about something that had been bothering me.

'And Rodolfo's father? I see that Rodolfo used the Argento family name, rather than adopting his father's. Was that for a reason?'

For a second or two, I saw that same expression of grief cross her face. 'I married late. Rodolfo was born when I was over forty, but his father died only five years later.' She glanced up at me and I could see the emotion in her eyes. 'Lung cancer. There was nothing they could do.'

'I'm so sorry to hear that. Was he involved with the agricultural business as well?'

'No, he was an opera singer. He wasn't a top-level singer like Rodolfo but I like to think that somewhere in his DNA was the origin of my son's amazing talent.'

'And what was his name?'

'Zoltan Nyisztor, he was Hungarian.' She spelled the name out to me. 'To be honest, it was for that reason that I kept Rodolfo with the Argento name. I could never think of my son as Hungarian.'

'Forgive me for returning to the will, but did your brother's children who run the company benefit from your son's will? You mentioned that Rodolfo owned a one-third share in the company. Presumably, that transferred to them.'

Her eyes hardened. 'Why should they get that? They already had their jobs for life.' There was a distinctly bitter note in her voice and I could imagine how frustrating it must have been for her to see the company handed over to somebody that she deemed not to have been up to the job. 'Rodolfo's share came to me.'

This was potentially fascinating. It sounded as though Violetta had done much better from her son's death than his cousins, who had in all probability expected to inherit his share in the business

– all thanks to the provisions of the will she herself had drawn up. 'How old are his cousins?'

She had to stop and think for a moment. 'Alfredo must be forty-two now, while Rosina is two years younger.'

'And they got nothing in your son's will?'

'Nothing, and they didn't deserve anything.' That hard look was back on her face again.

I did a bit of thinking. Violetta had provided me with the names of the two people who had stood to do very well out of her son's death: the wife and the agent. Alessia, the wife, had apparently inherited a hefty sum and the agent a million euros, which would have been a hefty sum to me and quite possibly to him as well. Even if Violetta might consider a million euros a paltry amount, his agent might have seen things differently and I had seen murders committed for far less in my time, so he definitely remained on my list of suspects. But there were also two others – the cousins, Alfredo and Rosina – who had probably hoped to inherit Rodolfo's share of the company, thus ridding themselves of the overbearing presence of Violetta. And this was before we even got into any question of rivals, enemies, jilted lovers – of whom there appeared to be no shortage – jealous husbands, or other people with a grudge. It looked as though I was going to have my hands full investigating the suspicious death of the famous tenor.

Any further conversation was interrupted by the arrival of the housekeeper, who informed us that lunch was served.

4

SUNDAY LUNCHTIME

We sat down to lunch in a huge, wood-panelled dining room housing a table longer than Violetta's car. She and I perched bizarrely at one end and the highly polished mahogany tabletop stretched away from us like a lane in a bowling alley. It could have held another twenty people comfortably. Although the temperature outside in the sunshine was now oppressively high, in here, protected by thick, stone walls, we were remarkably comfortable even without air con.

Considering how tiny Violetta was, I was blown away by the variety and volume of the food on offer and the amount she managed to consume. First, there was a huge platter of sliced ham, fennel-flavoured *finocchiona* and three other types of salami, accompanied by fresh figs and slices of luscious, orange-fleshed melon. Together with this, we had slices of the wonderful unsalted Tuscan bread smothered in chopped tomatoes and olive oil, and the housekeeper opened a bottle of very good Chianti Classico. This was followed by *pappardelle alla lepre*, the rich, gamey sauce extremely tasty, and I had to hold my hands over my plate to prevent the housekeeper from piling it high with even more pasta.

I like my food – not as much as Oscar, of course – but even I have my limits.

While we ate, we continued to talk, and I learned that Rodolfo Argento's death had taken place only a couple of kilometres from his home. As far as I could work out without a map, this was in the hills to the north of Verona, only a short drive from the historic city. I asked how long he had lived there and the answer was informative.

'The villa up there has been in the family since the end of the nineteenth century. My family is originally from Verona, but we have a number of houses dotted around Italy – in the high Alps, at the coast, and of course this villa here. I moved down here fifty years ago and I've stayed ever since.' She shot me a little smile. 'There's something about Tuscany.'

I pointed towards my plate. 'And Tuscan food. You have an amazing cook.'

'That's Teresa, she's a wonder. She's been working here since she was seventeen and I couldn't ask for a more perfect housekeeper.'

I nodded in agreement. 'You're very lucky. As for Tuscany more generally, I totally agree. I love everything about this part of the world.' I went on to query her a bit more about the family business and she elaborated.

'Like I told you, the family business is agricultural machinery and bulk agricultural products. We import and export everything from tractors and combine harvesters to milking machines and fertiliser. We also export Italian fruit and vegetables all over Europe. We've recently moved into wine as well and sales are developing nicely.' She then added almost casually, 'The company, Agri Argento, is the biggest in its field in Europe.'

Suddenly all the houses and all the millions were explained. 'And where's the company based? Verona?'

'Yes, the head office is there and we have a number of warehouses on the outskirts of the city, plus others dotted around Italy. My brother's children, Alfredo and Rosina, have always lived in Verona. Alfredo married about ten years ago and he's still married, although I'm not wild about his choice of wife.'

'Oh, why's that?'

She waved the question away. 'Oh, I don't know, there's just something about Ingrid, but maybe it's just because she's never liked me.' Considering Violetta's low opinion of her son's wife and now her nephew's wife, I wondered whether this antipathy might be more a reflection on the old lady's lack of tolerance than the fault of the younger wives.

'And the sister, Rosina, is she married?'

She shook her head. 'She was engaged to be married, but he was killed in a horrible skydiving accident. Why people have to choose to do such dangerous sports, I really don't know.'

I couldn't help a little spark of interest at another violent death affecting such a wealthy family and I resolved to check the death of Rosina's fiancé just in case. 'Are you in regular contact with Rosina and her brother? Will you be telling them you've hired me to investigate their cousin's death?'

She looked up from her food. 'I was going to tell Rosina – she and I have always been quite close. To be honest, I don't often speak to Alfredo. He's always a bit distant towards me and, like I told you, I've never been able to forgive him for not working as hard as he should. Do you think I should tell him about you as well?'

'I think you should, for one simple reason. I'm going to need to speak to both of them and, unless you tell Alfredo who I am, there's probably no way he'll agree to see me.'

She nodded slowly. 'Yes, I see. In that case, I'll certainly inform both of them.'

I was interested at her hesitation. She had said that she didn't speak to her nephew very often because he had always been 'a bit distant'. Was that just because she was down here in Tuscany and he was up there in Verona? Had he worked out that she didn't approve of his relaxed lifestyle? Alternatively, was it because of some rupture in the family – maybe caused by the wife who didn't get on with her husband's elderly aunt? I tried another line of questioning.

'What about relations between Rodolfo and his cousins? Was he on good terms with Alfredo and Rosina? Did they ever argue about business matters?'

She shook her head. 'Like I told you, he wasn't in the least bit interested in the business so that's why I acted for him. From the age of four, all he wanted to do was sing.' Her eyes were sparkling with maternal pride, tinged with raw emotion. Clearly, mother and son had been close. After a brief pause, she continued. 'But Rodolfo was on good terms with his cousins – he was friendly to everybody – and living in Verona, I'm sure he often met Rosina, although maybe not Alfredo.' She added a few words of explanation and her expression darkened. 'Alfredo's wife, Ingrid, is downright antisocial.'

'Did Alfredo resent having you looking over his shoulder when it came to the business?'

'I'm sure he did, but I had Rodolfo's one-third share to protect.' That hard tone was back again and I could easily see how relations between her and her brother's family might have soured.

'Out of interest, were the terms of your son's will common knowledge to all members of the family?'

A more cunning expression appeared on her face. 'I knew, of course, because I wrote Rodolfo's will – he had no interest in that sort of thing – but I'm sure it came as a surprise to the others. I know Alfredo was expecting to inherit Rodolfo's share of the company – and so was Ingrid, his wife. You should have seen the way both of them were looking daggers at me in the lawyer's studio when the will was read, passing Rodolfo's share to me, not them.' The expression on her face reflected a certain grim satisfaction and I realised – if I hadn't already – that beneath the 'elderly lady' façade lay a decidedly vicious streak.

I took refuge in a sip of the excellent Chianti as I reflected on what she'd said. I've never liked pre-judging people, but I couldn't help thinking that if one or the other of the two siblings had been hoping to inherit Rodolfo's share of the company, they might have individually or together engineered his 'accident'. His share of the company had now passed to Violetta so, if this were the case, might this mean that she could now be in danger? Presumably, as it was a family business, her interest in the company would ultimately revert to them if she also died. I looked around. With her all alone here in this isolated house with just a housekeeper and presumably a gardener, it wouldn't take a criminal genius to dream up a scenario that resulted in her death: a fall, a shock, a heart attack or even another car accident maybe. As she was at the venerable age of eighty-one, it was unlikely that anybody would delve too deeply into how it happened. I thought I'd better warn her of this possibility, but it's not easy to suggest that your close relatives might be considering murdering you, so I approached it obliquely.

'What are your plans for the next few weeks? Will you be here if I need to contact you?'

'That's something else I need to consider. I took a call yesterday from Rosina, telling me that they've called an extraordinary board meeting for next Friday and I suppose I should be there.'

'Where's that going to take place?'

'In the boardroom at Head Office in Verona.'

I didn't like the sound of this. If Alfredo and/or his wife or sister were intent on a second murder, Violetta would do well to stay as far from them as possible. Again, I tried a circuitous approach.

'Where do you stay when you go to Verona? With one of them?'

She shook her head. 'No, I stay at the villa. I have an apartment there. I know it so well and the staff there look after me.'

My ears pricked up at her mention of 'staff'. How big *was* the Verona villa? 'Who looks after the villa for you?'

'Dolores is the manager and she really runs things. She's Spanish and she's a treasure. She keeps everybody on their toes.'

'Everybody? Do a lot of people work there?' Having a 'manager' for a private house was odd.

I could see her pause to do a bit of mental arithmetic. 'Probably a dozen or so, maybe fifteen.'

I was obviously missing something unless her son had insisted on a different servant for every room of the house. 'And what do they all do?'

'They run the courses and look after the residents, of course.'

'But I thought you said your son was living on his own in his last few months.'

'I said that his wife had gone off gallivanting, but that didn't mean that he was left on his own.' Seeing the puzzled look on my face, she finally clarified the situation. 'I'm sorry, Signor Armstrong, I should have explained. When Rodolfo inherited the villa, he and I created a non-profit-making charitable trust and transformed the place – it's a very big building – into AOA, Accademia Opera Argento. We also transferred the villa to the trust so it wasn't part of Rodolfo's estate.' That ruthless expression was back on her face again. 'That way Alessia hasn't been able to get her hands on it. We wanted it to become the number-one conservatoire for opera stars of the future. Admission is fully sponsored by the trust so that everybody, regardless of their background, has the same equal opportunity. It's a charity that was very close to his heart, and I have every intention of keeping it going.'

This meant that Violetta intended to keep her dearly beloved son's memory alive, so there was an altruistic side to her after all. 'I see. And how many students are there at the villa now?'

'It's summer course time so I don't really know – twenty-five, thirty maybe – but you'll be able to see for yourself when you're staying there.'

The bamboozled look must have been back on my face but, luckily, she took pity on me. 'Don't worry, it's very comfortable, I can assure you. And of course you can take your lovely dog with you, as well as your history lecturer girlfriend.'

I looked across the table at her. Clearly, I wasn't the only detective in the room. 'You know Anna?'

She gave me a positively cheeky grin. 'I know *of* her. I drop into the café at Montevolpone at least once a week and I get all the local gossip from Monica. She speaks very highly of you and your girlfriend.'

I chalked one up to Violetta. She certainly didn't miss much, and this boded well for my chances of getting enough information out of her for me to reach a successful resolution to this case – and with another thirty possible suspects to add to my list, I was going to need all the help I could get.

I waited until the housekeeper had removed the remains of the pasta from the table and disappeared before I turned the conversation back to the matter in hand.

'As far as the day-to-day running of the company's concerned, do Alfredo and Rosina share the work? You said something earlier about it having been a mistake to make Alfredo the head of the company.'

A disapproving expression appeared on the old lady's face. 'Without Rosina, Alfredo would be lost.' Absently, she took a mouthful of wine, but I said nothing and waited for her to continue. 'Alfredo is the older of the two but that was incidental to my brother. He appointed Alfredo managing director simply because he's a man. Rosina didn't get a look-in.' A bitter note entered her voice and she looked up with an air of resignation about her. 'That's how it's always been in my family.'

'But you think Rosina would have done a better job than her brother?'

'Definitely. Of course she's a director of the company, but she ostensibly occupies a more junior role than her brother. In fact, I'm convinced that she's the brains behind the business and she does most of the work while he spends much of his time on the golf course.'

Before I could react to this, the door behind me opened again and the housekeeper reappeared, wheeling a trolley on which there was a huge leg of roast lamb, surrounded by a mountain of little roast potatoes. Unsurprisingly, I felt movement at my feet and Oscar's nose appeared by my knee, pointing unerringly towards the meat. I was pleased to see, however, that he resisted the temptation to make an all-out assault on the trolley and just stood there unsuccessfully trying to look as if he was in the latter stages of starvation. I handed him down a breadstick and he accepted it, although the look on his face made it clear what he would have preferred.

Over the roast lamb – which was cooked to perfection – we continued to talk and I learned more about the Argento family. Although they had always been commercially orientated, they had also maintained a long tradition of interest in opera. Violetta herself was named after the main character in Verdi's *La Traviata* and her son Rodolfo's name came from Puccini's *La Bohème*. Her brother had named his firstborn after Alfredo from *La Traviata*, and his daughter after Rosina, the heroine of Rossini's *Barber of Seville*. Violetta herself declared a lifetime interest in opera but added that she felt sure even Oscar could sing better than she did. What she didn't know was that when Oscar hears some of Anna's beloved opera music – particularly when sung by a soprano – he joins in and sings along. The result would no doubt make Maria Callas turn in her grave.

The good news about being able to stay in the Argento villa was that I should be able to find somebody there who would look after Oscar while Anna and I went to the Arena to hear our concert on Saturday. The thought of a howling Labrador interrupting the performance was too terrible for words.

5

SUNDAY AFTERNOON

I have to admit that when I got back from my monumental meal – the lamb had been followed by the most amazing tiramisu – all I felt like doing was collapsing onto the sofa and closing my eyes. Oscar, who had been served a massive bowl of leftover lamb and pasta by the cook, looked similarly afflicted and he stretched out at my feet with a deep sigh and was soon snoring happily. I was still asleep when Anna arrived at four-thirty and I was awakened by the sound of her car, but I must have still been looking dozy when she came in because she knew immediately what I'd been doing.

'Don't tell me: you had too much to eat and drink at lunchtime and you've been having a nap while I've been down in baking-hot Florence, sweating over a pile of dusty sixteenth-century books. It's all right for some.'

While Oscar hauled himself to his feet and trotted over to greet her, I made a beeline for the kitchen. 'A cup of tea or something cold?'

'Definitely something cold, but I don't know whether to drink it or pour it over myself. God, is it hot!'

I squeezed a couple of lemons, freshly picked from one of my own trees, and made her a big glass of lemonade with sparkling water from the fridge. I added sugar, threw in some ice cubes for good measure and took it across to her. 'Here, try some of this. I have some good news for you. I've managed to get us accommodation in Verona where we should be able to leave Oscar on Saturday night.'

She took the glass of lemonade from me and swallowed a big mouthful gratefully, before pressing the cold glass against her forehead. 'That is so good, thank you. Well done on finding the accommodation. Where is it?'

I went on to relate what I'd learned from Violetta Argento, and Anna listened with obvious fascination. In particular, when I told her that the Argento family's Verona villa was now an upmarket academy for opera singers, her eyes lit up. 'How wonderful! And we'll be staying there? I wonder if there will be any famous faces among them.'

I thought I'd better not build her hopes up too much. 'I doubt it; she said it's to promote and nurture talent for the future, so they'll probably be new faces to you. But, you never know...'

In spite of my doubts, there was a dreamy expression on her face now. 'Just imagine if they do their own concerts. We could have a front-row seat.'

'Best not with Oscar. Somehow I don't think his singing would be appreciated.'

She smiled back and reached over to ruffle Oscar's ears. 'Who knows? Maybe he'll suddenly develop a hidden talent. In fact, maybe you will too. Come to think of it, I don't think I've ever heard you sing. Do you maybe have a voice like José Carreras and you've been hiding your light under a bushel all these months?'

'Trust me, you don't want to hear me singing. Put it this way: Oscar is very definitely more tuneful than I'll ever be.'

She grinned and gave a theatrical shudder before returning to more practical matters. 'What's the plan? I'm pretty free next week, so if you want to go to Verona a few days earlier so you can get on with your investigation, I should be able to come with you. I've never been to the city before and there's a load of historical stuff I'm dying to see there.'

'Great, I told Signora Violetta that I'd have a word with you and then let her know. I also need to check with Lina, who controls my diary, but, as far as I can remember, there's nothing particularly urgent next week. Seeing as it's August, everybody's on holiday and even my customers are taking a bit of time off.'

Since I had set myself up as a private investigator, I had soon discovered that many of my cases were to do with marital infidelity, and the arrival of the month of August meant family holidays for most people, reducing the opportunities for adultery. I had no doubt that this would, inevitably, all start up again in September.

I'd been thinking about how long I would need to spend in Verona so I made a suggestion. 'If possible, I'd quite like to go up there on Wednesday. That would give me three clear days before the weekend. Would that be okay with you?'

'Fine by me.' She sat back and stretched her legs. 'And what about Violetta Argento? Are we giving her a lift? Don't tell me she's planning on driving that monster car of hers all the way to Verona.'

I'd been quite worried about that myself and had been heartened to hear Violetta say that she would take the train to Verona on Thursday in good time for the board meeting the following day. Impressive as the Bugatti was, I wondered how it – and she – would fare on a long journey up the autostrada. Certainly, if the old car were to break down, I felt sure the average roadside mechanic would be unlikely to have any suitable spare parts lying around. I was also still concerned about the possibility of an attempt on her life if, indeed, her son's death hadn't been an accident. Of course, that remained to be seen.

This brought me back to something that had been playing on my mind all day. From what I'd heard from Virgilio, there had been no signs of foul play when the experts had examined the wrecked car. If Rodolfo Argento really had been murdered, how could that have happened? A nearby witness had said that the car had made no attempt to brake and had just headed straight for the tree. Not for the first time, I had a feeling that, in spite of Violetta's suspicions, this might turn out to be suicide after all, but, if so, what might have pushed a handsome, successful, wealthy man with a new wife to end it all?

While Anna went upstairs for a cool shower to freshen up, I picked up my iPad and did a bit of online investigation. The first thing I checked was a highly specialised website dealing with the not too complex workings of classic cars. Unlike modern vehicles where mechanics often have to rely on computer diagnostics to discover faults and remedy them, cars over fifty years old aren't that different from cars of a hundred years ago: an internal combustion engine linked through a gearbox to four wheels and with a braking system inspired by that of the humble bicycle. Nowadays, there are all sorts of dual circuits and fail-safes, so the traditional would-be murderer's trick of simply cutting through a rubber or copper hose to drain the brake fluid no longer works. Not so for Rodolfo's 1967 E-type. Despite its sleek lines, the old Jaguar had been remarkably uncomplicated and, in consequence, more vulnerable than, say, my VW. But if somebody had fiddled with it, why had there been no trace of interference when the Verona police had examined it?

The next question was motive. Yes, I could see that the victim's two cousins might have been motivated to do away with the third shareholder in the hope of inheriting his share of the business, but why strike now? I would have to investigate whether they or his agent – who also stood to gain handsomely from the tenor's death – might have suddenly found themselves in urgent need of money for one reason or another. According to Violetta, it didn't appear that the company was having financial troubles, so it would almost certainly have had to be a personal matter and of course that opened the door to the killer being a woman – like his wife, for instance. I looked forward to talking to the four of them.

Other possible motives for murder can include love, lust and jealousy and I had a feeling I was going to be spoilt for choice with a raft of unhappy women apparently littering the singer's past. Professional jealousy, of course, could have come into it, as well as simple envy of him and his millions. There are some very bitter people out there and maybe one of them had taken a dislike to Rodolfo and decided to murder him. A check of his social media profile revealed lots about his career but very little of a personal nature. No doubt he'd been advised to steer clear of anything too intimate.

I sat down to read everything I could find online about Rodolfo Argento but it didn't tell me much that I hadn't already heard. His Wikipedia entry confirmed what I'd already been told and added very little. What were more interesting were a number of articles in scandal magazines about his outrageous behaviour, ranging from drug-fuelled sex parties to appalling treatment of a number of famous female stars, although there was no mention of him transgressing since getting married to Alessia. Otherwise, it was clear that he had been a rare talent, one of Italy's greatest tenors and, in spite of his relative youth, his name had been compared to the very best. Certainly, there appeared to be nobody sniping at him for poor performances.

I then turned my attention to his wife. When I checked her profile, I learned that Alessia Ricco, age thirty-seven, was a promising singer in her own right but, unexpectedly, not of classical music but of modern Italian music. Although pop prevails nowadays, Italy still embraces the ballad, and she was apparently making a name for herself on Italian television and at events such as the Festival of Sanremo, where she had appeared alongside well-known Italian crooners. Names like Ornella Vanoni and Massimo Ranieri probably mean little outside Italy, but to the locals, these singers still occupy legendary status. Listening to some of these is like stepping back in time to the days of Sinatra and the Rat Pack.

There were numerous photos of the glamorous wedding Alessia had enjoyed with Rodolfo on the island of Elba. Apart from her no doubt expensive wedding gown, other photos of her in glitzy and daringly revealing outfits on stage highlighted what an attractive woman she was. One wedding photo in particular, where she and Rodolfo were toasting each other with glasses of Champagne, showed her as an outstandingly beautiful woman and it was clear to a cynical old copper like me what had attracted him to her. No sooner had this thought crossed my mind than an echo of my ex-wife's voice reminded me that the attraction to Rodolfo didn't necessarily have to be lust. Surely it could just as easily have been her brain or her singing voice – but I remained unconvinced.

I could find absolutely no suggestion online of impropriety on her part as far as her marital vows were concerned, and in this day and age of paparazzi and investigative journalists, this was strange. Violetta had had no doubt in calling her out as unfaithful, but I could find nothing that backed up that assertion. Maybe the octogenarian had been mistaken or maybe she had deliberately been trying to cast doubt on the probity of her son's widow. I could well imagine that a new wife might not have gone down well with a protective *mamma* who had obviously been very close to her son, and slagging her off was Violetta's revenge.

When Anna reappeared, she was looking refreshed. She told me she'd skipped lunch and was starving but, seeing the expression of panic that flooded across my face – I was still feeling full from lunch – she took pity and suggested a solution.

'Why don't we go down to Tommaso and Monica's café? I'm sure Oscar will enjoy the walk and you look as though you have a few extra pounds to work off. We can sit outside in the shade and you can have a cold beer or two while I have one of her salads. She does a very nice tomato, basil and mozzarella salad with prawns.'

This struck me as an ideal solution and we set off down to the village on foot. It's a half-hour walk, but mainly on the *strada bianca* – so named because of the chalky white gravel coating on this, just like many of Tuscany's famous tracks – that snakes down the hill between ancient cypress trees that provide welcome shade. It was all downhill and so not very taxing, and by the time we decided to return, the sun would hopefully have lost some of its intensity and, in consequence, climbing the hill wouldn't be too much like hard work. As we walked, Oscar ran with us, collecting and bringing sticks and pine cones for us to throw for him. It was a delightful afternoon – as long as we stayed in the shade – and the view down over the valley of the River Arno to the deep green of the distant Apennines beyond was as charming as ever. I looked across at Anna and gave her a big smile.

'This is so far removed from my life in London that I can hardly believe my good luck. And that starts with you.'

She smiled back and pointed at Oscar. 'That's not strictly correct, though, is it? You met Oscar before you met me.'

I caught her hand and gave it a squeeze. 'Ah, but you can do things that he can't do for me.' I gave her a wink. 'Like cook, for example.'

Down at the café, most of the usual suspects were sitting in the shade discussing the usual topics. We chose a table not far from Giovanni the postman, and when he spotted me, he gave me a conspiratorial wave, beckoning me over. I left Anna with Oscar and went across to shake his hand.

'*Ciao*, Giovanni, what's new?'

He grinned up at me. 'How was your lunch with Signora Violetta?'

I was impressed. I had always known that the bush telegraph in Montevolpone was highly efficient, but this was above and beyond. I gave him a grin. 'It was excellent, thank you. I ate too much but it was worth it. So, go on, then, how did you know?'

He tapped the side of his nose in a conspiratorial fashion. 'A spy never reveals his sources. So, was it business or pleasure?' He then went on to demonstrate that he was totally wasted as a postman and probably would have done very well running the national security services for his country. 'You know what I think? I think she's employed you to investigate what really happened to her son. Am I right?'

I gave him an equally conspiratorial wink. 'A private investigator never reveals the identity of his clients.'

6

WEDNESDAY MORNING

The drive up to Verona on Wednesday was smoother than I had feared. We took the *Autosole*, the main north/south autostrada, up through the Apennines mountain range and then down onto the flatlands of northern Italy, forking east at Modena and passing the historic city of Mantua on our way to our destination. I had located the Argento villa on Google, and the satnav in my van steered me around Verona and onto the slopes of the first of the foothills of the Alps to the north of the city without too much trouble. We had been climbing for only ten minutes or so, and Verona was still in view below us, when I spotted our turn-off and swung left onto a minor road heading west around the flank of the hill to where the villa was situated. When we reached it, I saw that the entrance to the estate was through an impressive stone arch, firmly sealed by a pair of iron gates. A smart sign to one side indicated that this was the home of AOA, the Accademia Opera Argento. Interestingly, this was written both in Italian and in English, Argento Opera Academy. I pressed the call button on the gatepost and a disembodied voice rang out from the speaker.

'*Chi è?*' It was a woman's voice and it sounded friendly enough.

I gave her my name and was about to explain that I was a friend of Violetta's when there was the whine of an electric motor and the gates began to open. As they did so, the voice replied.

'Welcome to the academy, Signor Armstrong.'

Clearly, we were expected. By arrangement with Violetta, the only people here who'd been informed of my real purpose in coming to the villa were the manager, Dolores, and the principal, Clarissa. I didn't have their surnames. As far as anybody else was concerned, we were just friends of Violetta's here for a few days' holiday and a visit to an opera at the Arena. There would be time to reveal what I was really doing if I began to identify any possible suspects among the people here.

I drove in through the gates and the first thing we both noticed in the park surrounding the villa was the amazing view, not only south towards Verona and north into the high Alps, but west over the long expanse of Lake Garda, its blue waters dotted with sails as holidaymakers sought to escape the early-August heat.

After running across the top of a well-mown field with a pair of tennis courts at the far end, the drive disappeared briefly into a massive clump of rhododendron bushes before emerging into a gravelled parking area, beyond which stood the beautiful villa, now reborn as the opera academy. It was an amazing piece of architecture. Anna, ever the historian, had been researching its origins and she was able to tell me that it had been built at the end of the seventeenth century in the prevailing baroque style of the time. To my untrained eye, it reminded me of the Palace of Versailles that I'd visited with my wife and daughter twenty years earlier. I'm sure my gran would have described it as fussy, with its monumental pillars either side of the main entrance, its balustraded balconies and the mock-Roman statues positioned every three or four metres or so along the top of the façade concealing the roof. All around the parking area were meticulously maintained flower beds with a mass of magnificent roses in bloom and a huge area of lawn curving downhill beyond the flower beds. I could well imagine the effect coming here could have on aspiring opera singers. It must breathe new life into them.

There were no Bugattis or similarly valuable vehicles to be seen, so I presumed that Rodolfo Argento must have kept his collection elsewhere. Back in Tuscany, Violetta had told me that he had owned a dozen classic cars and I could only guess at how much a collection like that might be worth. Having had a number of elderly vehicles myself over the years, I know my way around old cars reasonably well but, of course, none of mine would have made it into Rodolfo Argento's collection – to a dump, probably, but definitely not of interest to a collector. I pulled up next to a nondescript Fiat, turned off the engine and checked my watch: eleven forty-five. I stretched and gave Anna a smile. 'Just in time for lunch.'

She shook her head in wonderment. 'I will never understand how you can eat as much as you do and never get fat.'

I grinned at her. 'Clean living and the love of a good woman. Possibly assisted by all those long walks I do with Oscar.'

Movement from the rear of the van told me that Oscar had realised that we were at journey's end and, more significantly in his eyes, that lunchtime was fast approaching. His nose appeared over the back of the rear seat as Anna and I got out and savoured the fresh air. It was still hot here but certainly not quite as overpoweringly hot as Florence. In particular, there was a very welcome breeze blowing, just hard enough to move the fronds of the row of magnificent palm trees planted around the parking area. I was mildly surprised to see palm trees up here so close to the high mountains but clearly this area had its own little microclimate. I opened the back of the van and Oscar jumped out, tail wagging happily as he headed for the nearest palm tree. I kept a watchful eye on him in case he decided to go charging into the flower beds, but he was just laying down a marker to all other dogs that he had arrived and was staking his claim to the villa and its grounds. He behaved impeccably and soon returned to accompany Anna and me across the gravel to the villa.

As we approached the entrance, a figure came out of the door and it was all I could do not to gape in amazement. He was a heavily built man, maybe in his sixties, and he was dressed in a striking outfit of green and black striped pantaloons, a salmon-pink and scarlet striped shirt and a three-pointed hat with bells at the corners. As it was, Oscar stopped dead and shot me an uncertain look that mirrored my bemusement. Fortunately, Anna left me looking gormless and walked over to the court jester character, holding out her hand.

'Rigoletto, I presume. I love your costume.' She addressed him in Italian and when he replied, I could hear his noticeable Tuscan accent. Maybe he was a Florentine just as she was.

The man, whose already red face had been embellished with traces of clown's make-up, smiled broadly and swept off his hat in a theatrical gesture, bowing low towards Anna as he greeted her in return.

'My pleasure, fair maiden... oh, shit.'

Now it was Anna's turn to look bemused. The jester was still bending towards her and I saw at once that he was having trouble straightening up so I hurried across to him and offered him a helping hand. He grabbed hold of my arm gratefully with both hands and slowly pulled himself back upright again, wincing as he did so.

'Thank you so much. Do excuse me, please. I'm afraid the doctor told me I shouldn't make any sudden movements but...' I saw a cheeky grin return to his face '...when confronted with such beauty, I couldn't stop myself.' He shot me a wink. 'That's the young lady I'm speaking about, not you, sir.'

I grinned back. 'I had already worked that out. I have to ask, do you always go around dressed like this or are you in the middle of a performance?'

'I most certainly do not go around dressed like this, but today is Verdi Wednesday.' Seeing the expression on my face, he explained. 'It was Dolores's idea: every Wednesday lunchtime, we dress up as characters from operas written by one of the great composers. Last Wednesday was Mozart, today's Verdi, next week it's Bizet and so on.'

Anna was looking enchanted. 'How wonderful. Do you all have your own costumes?'

'No, but Rodolfo used to collect operatic costumes as well as old cars. There's a huge selection here for us to choose from.' He smiled. 'It's a bit of fun, and it gives the students a taste of what might await them in the future.'

'And will *you* be singing some of Verdi's arias?'

He shook his head. 'Some of the others may well burst into song at some point – in fact, it's almost inevitable – but you wouldn't want to hear *me* sing. I can't sing a note. No, I teach stage-craft – you know, acting. So many of these kids come here thinking that opera is all about singing, but it's far more than that. Opera is a spectacle for all the senses, not just the ears.'

As he was sounding chatty, I gently mentioned the dead man. 'And this was all set up by Rodolfo Argento. How terrible that he's died. You must all miss him.'

Just for a moment, I thought I saw a shadow cross the jester's face, but then he immediately started nodding again. 'He was a very good man... well, maybe not such a good man if you happened to be a woman, but creating the academy was a master-stroke of generosity and I won't hear a word said against him.'

I exchanged glances with Anna. Clearly Rigoletto – or whatever his real name was – was confirming the womanising stories I had seen online and heard from Rodolfo's mother. Seeing as this man was apparently only too happy to talk, I tried quizzing him a bit more on the victim.

'He did have a reputation as a bit of a womaniser, didn't he? But I imagine most people here saw him as a benefactor.'

'He was a very generous man and everybody here owes him a lot.' A more serious expression appeared on his face. 'But not all of them are prepared to admit it.' Maybe realising that he had said too much, he sucked in an exaggerated lungful of air and gave us a little wave. 'Now I must go for my pre-prandial walk.' He smiled. 'Doctors? What do they know?' And he set off down the steps towards the lawn beyond the parking area.

Seconds later, as we were approaching the door ourselves, it opened and a woman appeared. She was wearing what looked like a medieval peasant woman's costume and she looked good in it. She was probably barely into her forties, with dark hair and a trim, energetic demeanour. There was a friendly smile on her face as she approached us but I found my attention attracted to her companion. Just as the door was about to close, it was nosed open by a very unexpected arrival. To my surprise, the woman was accompanied by a black Labrador, an inch or two smaller than Oscar but remarkably similar. Beside me, I suddenly saw Oscar register this new friend and a toothy canine smile appeared on his face. The woman, noting my surprise, made the introductions.

'You must be Signor Armstrong.' She glanced across at Anna. 'And this must be your partner but, I'm sorry, Signora Violetta didn't tell me your name or that of your lovely dog.' She pointed at the other dog, who was studying Oscar closely. 'I'm Dolores. I have the pleasure of being the manager of this wonderful establishment, and this is Elektra. I've had her for four years and she's very friendly.'

She shook hands with the two of us while at the same time bending down and patting Oscar's head with her free hand. She was obviously good at multitasking. Her Italian was excellent and if I hadn't been told that she was Spanish, I would never have guessed. She sounded as if she meant what she said about the villa. I couldn't detect even a hint of irony in her voice.

I was quick to confirm my identity and to introduce Anna and Oscar. For his part, Oscar wasted no time in trotting across to say hello to his mirror image. Elektra reached out with her nose and the two touched. The smile on Oscar's face grew even broader and the two dogs were soon giving each other a full olfactory check-up, tails wagging. While they were doing this and as we were outside in the open air and there was nobody else around, I took the opportunity to bring up the reason why I was here.

'I imagine that Signora Violetta has explained what I'm doing here. In spite of the conclusion arrived at by the police, she's convinced that her son was murdered. Do you have any thoughts on this?'

Dolores answered almost immediately. 'I honestly don't know what to think. Giacomo, who farms down the hill where the accident happened, saw the whole thing and the police said he confirmed that Rodolfo made no attempt to brake as he came to the corner. From the sound of it, I wondered if he'd had some sort of seizure. I find that hard to believe as he was still a young man, although he did have a tendency to push himself a bit too hard... Let's say he lived life to the full.' A vaguely disapproving look appeared on her face.

'I have a feeling I know what you mean by that, but could you maybe spell it out to me? I promise that when I submit my report, I'll be very careful to be as diplomatic as possible although, if you're going to say what I think, Violetta told me the very same thing a couple of days ago.' I caught her eye for a moment. 'Women?'

Her cheeks coloured and she nodded. Before replying, she glanced over her shoulder but the door behind her remained closed. The two dogs, tails still wagging, had clearly made friends and were sitting side by side, engaged in a silent conversation. Dolores, on the other hand, was struggling. 'It's just that...' She was looking more uncomfortable now and Oscar, who's far more sensitive than I am, got up and wandered over to lean against her leg in support. He was immediately followed by Elektra, who added her weight to Dolores's other leg. Encouraged by these signs of canine solidarity, she lowered her voice to little more than a whisper. 'I don't think there's a woman here who hasn't been groped by him at some time or other.'

Although I had already gathered that Rodolfo had been a womaniser, I had assumed that his relationships had been consensual. 'But didn't they mind? What about you? Were you a victim of his unwelcome advances?'

She was looking positively embarrassed now. 'I was and I told him to keep his hands to himself and, to be fair, he did. As far as the others are concerned, some did and some didn't.'

'I gather he had recently married. Do you think he might still have strayed a bit since?'

'It's not up to me to comment. Heaven forbid that I should sully the name of a wonderful, kind, generous man – and he really was all of those things.'

So there had obviously been another side to him as well. I gave her a few seconds before pressing her a bit more. 'I quite understand your position and your feelings, but please just answer me this: is it possible that he might have been carrying on with somebody here at the villa?'

She didn't look up from the dogs at her feet as she answered. 'It's possible, I suppose, but that's all I feel I can say.'

I couldn't help noticing that she hadn't poured cold water on the idea that Rodolfo might have had a relationship with somebody here, but I could sympathise with her position and I left it at that. 'He must have been quite a character.'

Dolores nodded. 'He certainly was that and, like I say, he lived life to the full; not just with his stage performances but skiing, sailing, climbing and, of course, racing his beloved cars. Certainly, I would definitely rule out suicide. He had everything a man could want.'

'What about his wife? Do you like her?'

I was mildly surprised to see her nod her head. Somehow, I'd been expecting more disapproval if Alessia had been unfaithful to her husband as Violetta had said. 'Yes, very much. She's a lovely friendly person and she's very talented – as well as being very beautiful.'

'And how did she and Rodolfo get on? Surely she must have realised that he was carrying on with other women?'

I was again surprised at what Dolores said next. 'She loved him dearly, I'm sure, and when they were together, they always looked happy.'

This was so totally different from what Violetta had told me that I had to find out more. 'I believe she's been away a lot, hasn't she?'

'She's really made a name for herself as a singer over the last few years and, of course, this has meant that she's been doing a lot of touring, with performances as far away as Argentina and the USA.'

'And of course Rodolfo was still doing quite a lot of touring himself, wasn't he? It must have been difficult for them to meet up.'

'Yes, indeed. But when they did, it was usually here – their haven away from the media. They looked really happy together right up until the end.' She looked up at me. 'So if you think she might have murdered him for his money, you should think again. Apart from the fact that I'm sure she has a lot of money of her own, she really loved him, I'm certain of it.'

'I'm sorry, but I have to ask: might she have been jealous if she thought that her husband was involved with other women?'

I had to wait for her answer. When it came, it sounded genuine. 'When she married him, she must have known what sort of man he was. I'm sure she knew he was a terrible flirt – or worse – but I'm equally sure that she didn't believe for a moment that once they were married, it ever went much further than flirting.'

I stood silent for a few moments and took stock. Yes, Rodolfo had been a womaniser, but it would appear that his marriage had changed him into a paragon of virtue. Call me an old cynic – and I am – but in my experience, such radical changes in behaviour are rare. Had this leopard really changed its spots? One thing was for sure: I was looking forward to talking to his widow.

No doubt anxious to get away from such a potentially intimate subject, Dolores glanced at her watch. 'Almost lunchtime. Why don't I show you to your suite?'

Oscar looked up with interest. She had mentioned lunchtime, after all.

7

WEDNESDAY LUNCHTIME

I'd been expecting a bedroom, no doubt a comfortable bedroom, probably with a private bathroom, but I hadn't been prepared for what greeted Anna and me on the top floor of the villa. When we emerged from the lift, we found ourselves on a broad landing with a beautiful marble staircase curling down to the lower floors straight ahead of us and a single door in the wall on the right-hand side. Unlike the other floors, which had had long corridors leading off in both directions, there was just a single corridor to our left. Dolores pointed to the right first.

'That's the entrance to Rodolfo and Alessia's apartment, and the corridor to our left leads to Signora Violetta's apartment and, beyond that, to the two guest suites.'

I decided to do a little bit more sleuthing. 'Is Alessia living here at the moment?'

Dolores shrugged her shoulders. 'She is and she isn't. Her official residence is still here and she was here last week, but she's been away since Friday performing in southern Italy. From what she told me before she went off, she should be back any day now.'

'That's good to hear. I'd be grateful if you'd let me know when she returns. I'll be interested to speak to her.'

Dolores led us down the corridor past Violetta's private apartment until we reached two more doors. She opened the first of these and ushered us inside. We followed the two Labradors into a large living area with a comfortable-looking sofa and armchairs and beyond that, a bedroom with a king-size bed and a luxurious bathroom. There were French windows in both of the main rooms, leading out onto the flat roof of the villa. Oscar and I wandered outside and I saw that these top-floor apartments were surrounded by a roof terrace that extended the full length of the building. Five metres in front of me, the terrace ended in a low wall with a fine statue of a scantily clad Roman maiden on it. I realised that this was the top of the façade and these apartments had been built onto the flat roof in such a way as to be hidden from the gardens below.

We had our own private piece of terrace, loosely divided from the other apartments by three large terracotta urns. Over the top of the façade, the views were magnificent. From here, we could see almost the full, deep-blue expanse of Lake Garda until it disappeared to the north of us into the distant Alps that rose steeply skywards, their peaks swathed in puffy, white clouds. Below us was the gravelled parking area surrounded by palm trees and rose beds. It was a delightful scene and Anna was obviously as impressed as I was because she turned to Dolores to thank her.

'This is amazing, thank you so much. It's absolutely gorgeous.'

Dolores smiled back at her. 'These top-floor suites are a bit special, but all the residents' rooms are really nice. For the students lucky enough to be chosen to come here, it's a wonderful environment in which to learn and progress.'

I joined in the conversation. 'Violetta told me you were running summer courses at the moment. How long do they last?'

And more importantly from my point of view, might any of the students or teachers be a potential murderer?

'Multiples of one month. A few students come just for one month but the majority come for the full summer term: July, August and September. Some come back year after year.'

'So would you say that most of the students here now have been here for at least a month?'

'Yes, all bar a handful. It's very competitive to get in here and students generally like to stay as long as possible.'

'And what sort of age are they?'

'Our youngest at the moment is Barbara from Munich – she's just nineteen – and the oldest is Michelle from Paris. She's almost my age, but the majority of them are in their twenties.'

'And how are students selected? I imagine a lot of people would give their eye teeth to get in here.'

'There's an application process and there's a panel who scrutinise all the applicants to select the most worthwhile. Clarissa, the principal, will be able to tell you more about the selection process, but what they're looking for is potential that can be developed. Rodolfo used to joke that he would never have been accepted as a student because by the time he was in his twenties, he was already an international celebrity.'

I felt a little ripple of disapproval run through me. One thing was clear: Rodolfo Argento could never be accused of having undervalued himself. The more I was beginning to hear of him, the less he resembled his mother's description of him as a wonderful human being. Of course, I reminded myself sharply, maybe this was just me being me. I've never liked what my old superintendent used to refer to as 'flash gits'.

Dolores glanced at her watch and changed the subject. 'I imagine Giorgio – the man in the Rigoletto costume – told you that we dress up on Wednesday lunchtimes. If you'd like to join in today, I can show you where the costume room is and you can pick something out.'

As Anna beamed, my heart sank. Still, I reminded myself, opera was Anna's thing and the least I could do was try to enjoy what obviously appealed to her, and if it meant dressing up in silly clothes, then so be it. It could have been worse – I could have been wandering around in the buff. Anna agreed happily and we followed Dolores out, this time down the magnificent staircase. We went down to the first floor where she took us to a far bigger room than I'd been expecting, lined with rails on which a multitude of colourful costumes were hanging. Dolores glanced at her watch again.

'I'll leave you two to pick something out for yourselves and to settle in.' She smiled. 'I'm sorry, but I don't think we've got any dog costumes.' I very nearly said, *Lucky Oscar*, but managed to stifle the instinct in time as she continued. 'Now I'd better get back to my duties. The dining room's on the ground floor, just past the bar. You can't miss it. Lunch will be served at twelve-thirty. I look forward to seeing you again then. Elektra, are you coming?'

The Labrador glanced at Oscar and then at Dolores before deciding to follow her mistress. For a moment, it looked as though Oscar felt tempted to follow her. Whether this was because he'd been smitten by this good-looking lady Lab or just because he thought she might lead him to his lunch remained to be seen.

We thanked Dolores profusely and she went out, leaving us surrounded by all the different operatic costumes in the slightly musty, museum-like atmosphere. Anna knew me so well by now and she came over, grabbed hold of my arm with her hands and looked up at me.

'You don't really mind dressing up, do you, Dan? It will be fun, I promise.'

I told her that I was happy if it made her happy, and we set about looking for costumes while Oscar developed considerable interest in a basket on the floor containing wigs and false beards. I wondered idly whether he thought there might be a squirrel in there. Luckily, Anna decided to go with one of Verdi's most popular operas, *Il Trovatore*, for our costumes. When I say luckily, this is because the opera is set in early-nineteenth-century Spain, which meant that I didn't need to wear tights. On previous occasions when we'd dressed up, the costumes had belonged to the medieval period, and tights and pantaloons have never appealed to me – or suited me. As it was, I picked up a baggy peasant blouse thing and a red neckerchief, accompanied by a broad leather belt complete with scabbard and remarkably convincing-looking wooden dagger. On top of a pair of black jeans, the ensemble would probably look okay. Needless to say, Anna fully entered into the spirit of the thing and picked herself out a beautiful purple dress and a gilded necklace studded with jewels that, if real, would have been worth more than this villa.

I went out to the van and collected our bags along with Oscar's basket and all-important food bowl and took them back up to our luxury suite. By the time I'd fed him and we'd changed into our operatic personae, it was almost half past twelve, so we headed downstairs for lunch. The dining room was enormous and I counted at least a dozen tables dotted about, most already full of people in colourful costumes. Clearly, everybody had entered into the spirit of Verdi Wednesday. Anna and I stopped at the door and looked around, and we were trying to work out where to sit when a woman wearing an extravagant, off-the-shoulder, blue gown waved to us to go across to her table. We did as requested and found her sitting with a man in Renaissance costume. As he turned towards us, I saw that he was a handsome black man and these were all the clues that Anna needed. She smiled at them both.

'Lord Othello, Lady Desdemona, how wonderful to meet you.'

Desdemona beamed at her. 'How charming you look, my dear.' She glanced across at the Othello character beside her and gave him a wry smile. 'That is the exact same dress that I wore at La Fenice almost twenty years ago.' She sighed nostalgically. 'The mayor of Venice said mine was the finest rendition of "Tacea la Notte Placida" he'd ever heard.' It was pretty clear that this woman wasn't the kind to hide her light under a bushel either. Maybe opera singers had boasting in their genes. After giving me and my costume an appraising look – I wasn't sure how impressed she was – she returned her attention to Anna. 'What's your name, dear?'

Anna introduced the two of us and went up even further in my estimation when she correctly identified Desdemona by name as Valentina Russo. I wouldn't have had a clue. It was clear that the lady was delighted to be recognised and she beamed back at us.

'The dress fits you so perfectly, my dear. I'm afraid I wouldn't stand a chance of getting into it now. I work here in the summer as a voice coach. Are you new arrivals? Would you two like to join us for lunch along with your lovely dog?'

Anna explained that we were friends of Rodolfo Argento's mother and an expression of grief passed across the singer's face. Close up, she was probably in her early sixties and the skin of her face was remarkably – maybe suspiciously – smooth and wrinkle free. No doubt she was still more than capable of wowing the opera-going public. The Othello character alongside her was probably ten years younger than she was and he appeared happy to stay in Valentina's shadow. We accepted their kind invitation to join them and I discovered that Othello himself was in fact an American called Luther Green and he spoke excellent Italian as well as English with a strong, southern-states accent.

While Anna and Valentina chatted – mostly about Valentina's operatic triumphs – I got to know Luther Green. He told me that he'd moved to Italy from Atlanta, Georgia, at the age of twenty and had lived and worked here ever since. He told me he rarely went back to the States nowadays and indicated our comfortable surroundings with a sweep of his hand.

'Why would I wanna leave a place like this? These folks saved my life and I'd do anything for them.' In response to my quizzical look, he explained. 'A few years back at the age of forty-nine, I developed throat cancer. I was very lucky that it didn't kill me, but at the time, I found myself wishing it had done. It robbed me of the most important thing in my life: my voice. In the space of a couple of months, I went from encores for my starring role in Mozart's *Marriage of Figaro* at the Teatro dell'Opera in Rome to spitting blood and croaking like a frog.' He looked up at me and I could read the anguish still inside him. 'No, worse than a frog. I couldn't make a sound.'

'And Rodolfo helped you?'

His expression changed to one of considerable warmth. 'Like I told you, Rodolfo saved me. He helped me through the worst time of my life and then two years ago, he and Clarissa offered me a teaching position here and it's opened up a whole new career for me. Since then, I haven't looked back.'

'And your voice?'

I was pleased to see him smile. 'I used to be a bass, a real deep, second F bass. I could set all the bottles in the bar shaking with my rendition of "Non più andrai". They called me the new Boris Christoff.' I thought it better not to tell him that I'd never heard that name before and had no idea what second F meant, but that definitely said more about me than about the opera singer. Unaware of my ignorance, he continued wistfully. 'Now I sound like a weak tenor, at best.'

Which was still a heck of a lot better than me. I offered some consolation. 'But at least you got your voice back.'

'Yeah, and I ended up here among some of the most wonderful folks in the world.' For a moment, a shadow flitted across his face. 'Not all of them, of course, but most of the kids who come here are amazing.'

I was filing away this little note of discord for future investigation when the conversation was interrupted by the arrival of a steaming tureen of vegetable soup and a basket of bread rolls. The waitress also put a litre carafe of red wine and a bottle of water on the table in front of us before wishing us *'buon appetito'* and moving on to the next table. On a hot day like today, soup wouldn't have been my first choice, but it tasted good and I spooned it up willingly while listening to Valentina Russo.

It soon became clear that we had found ourselves an excellent guide. Valentina knew everybody and, when I say she knew everybody, this extended far beyond their names. With only the slightest encouragement from me, she was soon giving us a detailed warts-and-all description of the people around us. Apart from four other tutors, it looked as though the majority of the diners were of student age or just a little older and they came in all shapes and sizes and from all ethnic groups. I felt sure that the atmosphere here must be exciting and stimulating for those chosen. As I looked around, I estimated that the students were roughly half male and half female, and a number of the women were remarkably good-looking. Whether this was just the luck of the draw or whether they had been selected on the basis of Rodolfo's particular inclinations remained to be seen. As my ex-wife never ceased to tell me, I've always had a suspicious streak.

I listened closely, wishing I could record all the names and nationalities – they came from all over the world – in my notebook but preferring not to look too inquisitive for now. I couldn't help noticing a look of disapproval on Valentina's face when she mentioned one young man in particular. His name was Romeo and she told us he came from just down the road in Vicenza. As diplomatically as possible, I followed the direction of her eyes and tried to elicit a bit more information about him.

'Is that Romeo over there, dressed as a shepherd?'

'That's him, charming the girls as always... living up to his name.'

I could see that the man in question had positioned himself at a table with three particularly pretty girls. From what I could see of him, he was a good-looking guy and certainly the three women with him looked happy in his company. This made me wonder whether maybe he might have struck up a relationship with one or more of the women here. If that were the case and if Rodolfo had subsequently directed his own attentions at that woman, might this have caused jealousy on Romeo's part, leading to murder? Anything was possible.

Valentina also pointed out the two women Dolores had mentioned: Michelle from Paris, the oldest of the students at the ripe old age of thirty-seven, and the youngest, Barbara from Munich, who was a mere nineteen and outstandingly beautiful. Even from some distance, I could see that she was a stunner and I couldn't help being suspicious of Rodolfo's motives once again. Might he have granted her a place on the course so he could have an affair with her and might this have caused jealousy and a murderous reaction from somebody here – even his wife?

My musings were suddenly interrupted by a voice at the far end of the room. And what a voice! A big man had suddenly stood up from his table. He was probably not yet thirty, but with his height and considerable bulk, he could have been a rugby player. He was wearing a sober, dark waistcoat over a white shirt trimmed with lace and he began to sing, slowly at first and then speeding up. His voice echoed throughout the whole room as he sang for about three or four minutes before the aria came to what sounded like a tragic climax. As he fell silent, the room erupted into applause and Anna and I joined in. Thankfully, Oscar had resisted the temptation to join in and I was relieved but, as I say, it's normally sopranos who do it for him. Beside me, Luther gave me a few words of explanation, his expression a mixture of pride and regret.

'That's Amadeo Gramsci. Give him time, but I believe he's going to become one of the greatest bass voices of all time. He's one of our star pupils. People say I used to sound like him...' His voice tailed off into melancholy but I was quick to cheer him and keep him talking.

'That was amazing. You must be so good if you sounded like that. Tell me, what's the name of the piece he was singing?'

'It's Verdi, of course. It comes from his Don Carlos and it's called "Ella giammai m'amò". It's a classic.'

I glanced across at Anna. 'That was terrific. I'm really looking forward to my trip to the opera on Saturday night.' And, to my considerable surprise, I realised I meant it.

The soup was followed by braised beef in a red wine sauce accompanied by roast fennel with parmesan. Both were excellent. According to Valentina, the wine was Valpolicella, produced from the villa's own vineyards. Finally, we were served *zuppa inglese* – Italy's take on trifle – followed by powerful espresso coffee. I couldn't fault the food or the service and I could well see how the guests here could justifiably praise Rodolfo Argento for his incredible generosity. Inveterate womaniser and 'flash git' he might have been, but nobody could have doubted his charitable nature.

It was a very enjoyable meal but it ended rather abruptly for me. Just as I was finishing the last of my coffee and thinking about taking Oscar for a good walk, another future opera star suddenly stood up only a couple of tables away from us and launched into song. This was a delightful aria but there was just one problem:

the woman singing had a very high-pitched voice and within a few seconds of her starting, I knew there was going to be trouble. There was a sudden movement at my feet and the next thing I knew, I had a pair of hairy Labrador paws resting on my thighs as Oscar raised his nose to the heavens – unfortunately only a few inches from my ear – and joined in. I hastily jumped to my feet, waved a quick farewell to our companions, and headed for the door, ears ringing, dragging my howling Labrador behind me.

8

WEDNESDAY AFTERNOON

Anna waited to hear the end of the aria and then came out to join us. She told me it had been 'Sempre Libera', one of the most famous of all of Verdi's works and it came from *La Traviata*. It had been sung to perfection by the soprano although I felt that the attempted intervention by my dog probably hadn't helped. Anna told me she had apologised to the young singer on Oscar's behalf and had been given an indulgent smile in return. Even so, I knew I was going to have to keep an eye on him while we were here.

Anna told me she had some work to finish so Oscar and I went for a walk on our own – but only after I'd changed back into normal clothes again. I wanted to see exactly where the accident had taken place and I didn't fancy wandering down a country road dressed as a character out of a Thomas Hardy novel. I checked with Dolores before leaving so as to be sure exactly where I could and should go. She told me that the estate extended as far as a clump of woodland to the north of the villa and I decided to start there and then curl back around so as to take in the vineyards on the west-facing hillside above Lake Garda and the scene of the crash. Elektra seemed remarkably happy with Oscar so I offered to take both dogs with me, and Dolores was only too happy to accept.

'She needs a good walk. I've been particularly busy this week so she hasn't been out as much as usual. Don't worry about a lead. She'll trot along with you quite happily and she's good with cars.'

Shortly after setting out, I came across a man sitting on a tractor, about to start mowing the lawns beyond the villa, and I stopped to say hello. He looked as though he was around my age, with a weather-beaten face, and he seemed only too willing to talk. After a brief discussion about what sounded like a very comprehensive irrigation system up here to keep the grass looking so good, I gradually managed to bring him around to the subject of the recent tragedy and he shook his head sadly.

'Signor Rodolfo was a good man, a very good man. Such a pity.'

I decided to be as tactful as possible in my approach. 'I've been hearing that some people think it might not have been an accident.'

He shot me a sceptical look. 'Well, I can tell you this: it certainly wasn't suicide. I was helping him work on the engine of his lovely old Ferrari Dino only the day before the accident and he was as happy and cheerful as ever. He was telling me something about going to Venice at Christmas to perform in front of kings and queens.'

'He used to work on the cars himself?'

'Yes, for the fairly straightforward stuff, but when it came to major work, he always used Maurizio down in Verona.'

'Maurizio?'

'Maurizio Tamburo, he has a garage specialising in classic cars.'

'What time of day was it when the accident happened? Was there good visibility?'

'It was just after lunch and the sun was out – like today. He told me he was going down to the lake for a walk after lunch.'

'Was that something he often did?'

'To be honest, no, not really. Only when he needed to clear his head – like after an argument.'

'Had he had an argument with anybody that lunchtime?'

He shrugged his shoulders. 'I've no idea. He didn't say anything to me, although he wasn't smiling.'

This fact went straight into my mental notebook as worthy of further investigation. Had there been an argument and, if so, with whom and about what? 'Where did the accident happen?' By now I could see him eyeing me suspiciously. It was clear he thought I was asking far too many questions but, at least for now, he didn't query why.

He swivelled on the tractor seat and pointed downhill in the direction of the lake. 'Less than a kilometre down there. There's a long, straight bit of road with a nasty right-hand bend at the end. Giacomo – he farms that land – saw the whole thing. He said the E-type came down the road like a rocket and just ploughed into the big old cypress tree and caught fire. I went down to take a look that afternoon before they took it away and the car was almost unrecognisable. You could hardly tell that it had once been a car at all. I shudder to think what state his body must have been in.'

'You say Giacomo is the farmer who works the land down there?'

'Yes, you can see his farm from here.' He pointed and I could just see the red tiled roof of a farmhouse alongside two huge trees. That should be easy to find. I tried a more direct question.

'Do you think it's possible that somebody tried to murder him?'

He looked across and shrugged helplessly. 'Don't think I haven't been asking myself the exact same question. The thing is, how could it have happened? That Jaguar was almost sixty years old, but it was in beautiful condition and he was always fiddling with it or just polishing it. Maurizio gave it a full service only a couple of months ago so there can't have been anything seriously wrong with it. Besides, if somebody had been tampering with the brakes, surely the police would have noticed when they investigated the accident – although, like I say, there wasn't much left to examine after the crash and the fire.' He was still looking closely at me and a hint of a smile appeared on his face. 'So what are you: police, secret service, insurance investigator?'

I smiled back and decided not to prevaricate. 'All right, you've got me. I have a private investigation agency and Rodolfo's mother is convinced that his death was suspicious. She's asked me to look into it and so far, the only people who know why I'm here are Dolores, Clarissa the principal, and now you. Could I ask you to keep it to yourself for a day or two?'

'Of course.' He seemed pleased to be included in the secret. 'If somebody really did murder Signor Rodolfo, you can count on my 100 per cent cooperation.'

'Thank you very much. By the way, my name's Dan Armstrong.' I pulled out my notebook and started to take notes. 'Could I have your name, please?'

'Giuseppe Pavese, but everybody calls me Beppe.'

'Thanks, Beppe. Have you worked here long?'

'Thirty-three, no, thirty-four years. I started looking after the grounds when the villa was still just a private house. My father worked for the Argento family for forty years before me.'

This sounded promising. He'd obviously been here since before the villa had changed to its current use and so he probably knew as much about this place as anybody. Also, if he had worked here so long, it made it less likely that he would suddenly have decided to murder his boss. Not impossible, but unlikely.

I decided to find out more about Rodolfo's classic car collection. 'You could maybe start by telling me where Rodolfo kept his cars. Presumably under lock and key?'

He pointed towards the rear of the villa. 'Some years ago, he converted the old stables into the garage for the cars. It's like a museum in there, the cars all lined up side by side.'

'How many cars are there in the collection?'

'Twelve… eleven now. One more beautiful than the next.'

'What happened to the wreck of the Jaguar? Is it still with the police?'

He shook his head. 'I saw Maurizio the other day and he told me he'd been asked to pick it up from the police pound and take a look at it for them – presumably checking for signs of tampering. It's in his garage now and he's also been asked to see if there's any chance of rebuilding it, although I'd be amazed if there's anything worth saving.'

'Surely the police wouldn't have asked him to do that?'

'No, that was Alfredo, Signor Rodolfo's cousin. Have you met him?'

'Not yet, what's he like?'

He glanced around before answering. 'To be honest, he's a bit of a pain. Don't quote me on that. Let's just say that the most important person in Alfredo's life is Alfredo. Not like his sister – she's always got a friendly word for everybody and she's definitely got her head screwed on, that one.'

'That would be Rosina? She's more clued up than he is?'

'Without her, he'd be lost. He only seems to be interested in golf and fast cars.' He shook his head ruefully.

This confirmed what Violetta had told me, but I stuck with cars for now. 'How do I get access to Rodolfo's garage with all his cars?'

'I have a key. I can let you in any time.'

'Does anybody else have a key?'

'Dolores has duplicates of all keys in the safe, and of course Signor Rodolfo had one, but I don't know who's got that one now.' He looked up and shook his head. 'I very much doubt whether it survived the crash and the fire. I think his mother, Signora Violetta, also had a copy because she sometimes drove some of his cars.'

'Who else has access to the safe apart from Dolores?'

He shook his head. 'Clarissa might have, I imagine, but otherwise I'm afraid I don't know. You'd have to ask Dolores that.'

I glanced at my watch. It was just after two. 'I'm going to take Oscar and Elektra for their walk now and check out the scene of the accident while I'm at it. If I see the farmer, I'll stop and have a chat to him but I should be back here by half past three or so. What time do you go off?'

'I'm normally here until five but I can stay longer if you like.'

'Thanks, but I'm sure that won't be necessary. Maybe when I come back, you could let me into the garage so I can have a look around.'

I continued with our walk as far as the little piece of woodland, where Oscar was able to find a host of sticks for me to throw for him to fetch. Elektra, on the other hand, just selected a suitably appealing branch and carried it with her, refusing my offers to take it from her and throw it. Unfortunately, her chosen branch was almost four feet long and she appeared blissfully unaware that every time she turned her head, she risked tripping me up. The breeze up here on the hillside was very welcome and in the shade of the trees, the temperature was perfect. From the woods, we headed down through a well-tended vineyard in the direction of the lake. There were already well-formed bunches of grapes on the vines that would, no doubt, produce next year's supply of Valpolicella for the villa.

We carried on downhill until we came to a road. From the direction of it, this was pretty evidently the continuation of the one we had taken to get to the main gates of the villa and I could see what Beppe had meant about a long straight ending in a sharp bend. I could well imagine the opera singer gunning the Jaguar down here without a care in the world.

Until he reached the bend.

We walked down the quiet country road without meeting a single vehicle and finally reached the scene of the accident. Even without the extensive damage to an old timber fence and the burn marks on the massive trunk and lower branches of an ancient cypress tree on the edge of another vineyard, I could see quite clearly that this was the scene of the crash. I estimated there to be well over a hundred faded floral tributes stacked around the tree where grieving fans had come to pay their last respects. It was a touching scene but the detective in me was far more interested by what I couldn't see. Looking back up the road, I couldn't see even the slightest hint of a skid mark and the E-type had been built years before anti-lock braking had been invented. The farmer who'd seen the crash had been dead right. Either Rodolfo hadn't tried to brake, or his brakes had failed.

My attention was then drawn to the sound of a vehicle coming up through the vines and I spotted one of those funny little narrow tractors that pop up in vineyards all over Italy. Driving it was an elderly man, and I took a chance. I flagged him down and climbed through the gap in the fence to speak to him, accompanied by the two dogs.

'Good afternoon, are you Giacomo by any chance?'

He reached forward and switched off the noisy engine. 'I am indeed. How can I help you?'

I decided that, just like with Beppe, I was going to have to take him into my confidence. 'My name is Armstrong. I've been asked to investigate the circumstances surrounding Rodolfo Argento's death and I believe you witnessed the crash.'

To my relief, he didn't question my presence and appeared keen to help. 'Like I told the police, the Jaguar just came roaring down the road, straight into the tree, and exploded. I bet he was doing ninety or a hundred. He never touched the brakes or, if he did try them, they weren't working.'

'Could you see the driver's face?'

He shook his head. 'I only caught sight of the car at the very last moment, I'm afraid.' He shuddered. 'You should have seen it after it hit the tree. Awful!'

'Did he hit the tree straight on?'

'Not quite. He must have turned the wheel because the front left-hand wing took the worst of the impact and, of course, that's where he was sitting.'

'And were the police the first people to arrive?'

'Yes, along with the ambulance and the fire engine. I phoned the emergency services immediately after the crash and I suppose it took them about twenty minutes to reach the scene. Luckily by that time, I'd managed to beat the worst of the flames out but there was nothing I could do for Rodolfo.'

'He was killed in the impact?'

He just nodded grimly. 'No doubt about it. His body was in a terrible state.' His bleak expression said it all.

We chatted a little more but it was clear that he had told me all he knew. Finally, I thanked him and set off up the road again with my two canine companions. As we made our way back through the vineyard towards the villa, I reflected on what I'd just heard. It was clear to me that the most likely explanation for the accident had to be brake failure. The fact that the Jaguar hadn't hit the tree straight on indicated that Rodolfo had been trying to steer into the bend or, at the very least, had been doing his best to avoid hitting the massive tree. To my mind, this made it clear that he'd been trying to take avoiding action, and so Dolores's theory of a seizure didn't stand up unless it had been a fleeting attack of some kind from which he'd awakened at the very last moment. It would be interesting to see whether he had a history of epilepsy or similar but, if not, it still looked like brake failure to me. The attempt at avoiding action would also indicate that it hadn't been suicide unless, of course, that had been his plan but he'd lost his nerve at the last moment and spun the wheel in a vain attempt to avert the inevitable.

I added an urgent trip to Maurizio's garage to my to-do list. Maybe the mangled remains of the Jaguar might still provide a clue.

9

WEDNESDAY AFTERNOON

When I got back to the track by the villa, I found that Beppe had finished mowing the extensive lawn and was taking a break in the shade of a big old chestnut tree. Elektra, still proudly carrying her branch, set off for the villa without a backward glance, while Oscar stood and watched her all the way until she disappeared from view. I definitely got the impression that love might be blooming here so close to Shakespeare's most romantic city, and I glanced down at him.

'Parting is such sweet sorrow, isn't it, old buddy?' I studied *Romeo and Juliet* at school and I still remember a few lines.

Oscar turned back towards me, wagged his tail slowly, and together we went over to Beppe where I asked if it would be convenient for him to show me the garage. He agreed immediately and led me around the side of the villa to a long, red brick building, at the end of which was a wide, modern, up-and-over double garage door. He produced a remote control from his pocket, pressed it and the door hummed up, revealing an Aladdin's cave of precious old vehicles.

I was faced with an amazing selection of classic cars lined up in echelon formation, noses pointing towards the door, with a gaping empty space at the front, presumably where the Jaguar had lived before the accident. I walked down the central gangway, admiring each of them as I went past. Although I probably couldn't name more than two or three of the individual models, I immediately recognised the legendary badges on the bonnets, ranging from the prancing horse of Ferrari to the Mercedes three-pointed star and the beautiful silver statue of a flying lady on the front of an immaculate, pure-white Rolls-Royce roadster. Along the rear of the huge room was a workbench equipped with tools of all description, in front of which was what looked like a fully functioning hoist, so cars could be raised in the air when access was needed from below. Certainly, it looked remarkably well equipped for an amateur workshop and I had little doubt that the cars had indeed had a terrific amount of care and attention lavished upon them. This of course made a faulty braking system even less likely and deliberate sabotage more probable. I turned to Beppe, who was absently wiping a speck of near invisible dust from the hood of a gleaming, ancient Maserati.

'Who was allowed to drive these vehicles? Was it just Rodolfo or was there anybody else? Did you drive them?'

'I've driven all of them, but only for short distances to check something we'd been working on. The only one I've had the use of for any length of time was the Rolls-Royce. When my daughter got married, Signor Rodolfo very kindly let me borrow it for the day to drive her to and from the church.'

'Were you the only other one to drive them?'

He shook his head. 'His wife used to love driving the Jaguar.'

'She's interested in classic cars?' This was probably a very sexist thought on my part but somehow, I had always associated classic or vintage cars with men, rather than women drivers.

Clearly, given that Violetta was also an enthusiast, this wasn't the case.

'She's *very* interested. In fact, Rodolfo told me they met at a classic car rally. She owns the most beautiful 1964 Porsche 911, one of the first to be built, and they kept it in perfect condition.'

'They?'

'She and Signor Rodolfo together. It was a shared passion of theirs.'

'She knows her way around cars?'

'Not as well as he did, but yes, she was quite happy to get her hands dirty.'

This was potentially very interesting. If the brakes of the Jaguar really had been tampered with, it must have been done by somebody with a reasonable working knowledge of car mechanics. From the sound of it, Alessia fell into that category. I was certainly looking forward to questioning her.

'Anybody else drive the cars?'

'Signora Violetta from time to time, and Alfredo was occasionally allowed to drive one or two, but he's a crazy fast driver. His father, Carlo, who died some years ago now, always felt that Alfredo didn't show the appropriate respect for the classic vehicles. In fact, it was interesting that when Carlo died, he left the collection of cars to Rodolfo rather than to his own son. It was Carlo who first started the collection – it was a real obsession of his – and Rodolfo subsequently added the Ferrari and the Rolls-Royce. They were the only people to drive the cars and, otherwise, nobody had access to them.'

'And you're sure that nobody else had a key to this place apart from you, Violetta, Alessia and Rodolfo, and the one in Dolores's safe?' He nodded and I added the obvious corollary to this. 'Is there any way the E-type might have been elsewhere on the day of the accident or the day before where somebody could have tampered with it?'

'Certainly not the day before. It rained all that day and none of these cars have ever seen a drop of rain since they were brought here. Carlo and then Rodolfo only ever took them out when it was dry.'

'And the morning of the accident?'

He had to stop and think. 'I was weeding the rose beds outside the front of the villa that day and I remember Signor Rodolfo going off with his wife in her Porsche mid-morning. From the racket it was making, it was obvious there was a hole in the exhaust and they went off to buy a new part. They were only out for an hour or so, but while they were away, Alfredo turned up to show off his brand-new Lamborghini.'

'Do you think *he* might have gone anywhere near the garage?'

'He didn't get out of the car. Besides, even if he had done, I bet he wouldn't even have known how to open the bonnet. Alfredo isn't the sort of person who likes getting his hands dirty. He called me over and asked me if Rodolfo was in, and when I told him he'd gone out, he just snorted and drove off. He's like that, Alfredo.'

'I don't suppose you have any idea where he went, do you?'

He shook his head. 'All I can tell you is that he headed towards the lake because I could hear his car screaming down the straight as he did so.'

'When was the last time the E-type was driven before the day of the accident?'

'I've been trying to work that out. It was unusually rainy at the beginning of July so it probably hadn't been out for at least a couple of days.' He caught my eye. 'I know what you're thinking – somebody might have got in here and tampered with the brakes, but how? There are very few keys and it wasn't me, so who?'

Who indeed?

I took a good look around, checking the two side doors and all the windows, which were firmly closed and bolted. Had one of these been left open a month ago, maybe because of the heat, allowing the murderer to get in to tamper with the Jaguar? Anything was possible but, after so much time had passed since the accident, there was no way of checking up now. Finally, I thanked Beppe, and Oscar and I went back to the villa and up to our room where we found Anna just finishing off her work. She looked up at me enquiringly.

'Well, Sherlock, did you find out anything interesting?'

I told her what I'd learned from Beppe and the farmer and explained how I was ever more convinced that it hadn't been an accident or suicide. I didn't need to spell it out for her.

'So you're saying that you think it really was murder?'

'I can see no reason on earth why he would have wanted to take his own life and, although there's still the unlikely possibility of it having been some sort of temporary seizure, yes, I think his mother might be right and it was murder.'

'What are you going to do about it – go to the police?'

I'd been thinking about this myself. 'Yes, but not yet. All I have at the moment is conjecture. I need something more concrete. Violetta gave me contact details of the two cousins who run the family business so I'll get in touch with them now and see if I can make appointments to speak to them tomorrow. I also want to visit the classic car garage, which apparently now has the remains of the Jaguar. I'd like to see what the mechanic there says about any possible mechanical fault. It sounds as though Rodolfo's widow, Alessia, is a classic car enthusiast and she's due back any day now, so I'll wait until I've spoken to all of them before I consider going to the police. Do you have any particular plans for this evening?'

She shook her head. 'No, I've done what I needed to do, so I'm in your hands completely.'

'Great. In that case, I'll fix up the appointments and then I'd like to take a drive past the scene of the accident to the lakeside. Dolores told me there's a café down there that the victim sometimes frequented. You never know, there might be people there who can shed some light on what happened or, more particularly, why it happened. After that, I need to check out the classic car garage and then, if you like, why don't we head for the city centre for a quick look at the main historic sights before coming back here for dinner and a bit more sleuthing. Okay?'

I dialled the number Violetta had given me for the brother and sister who ran Agri Argento and spoke to their PA. It was immediately clear that Violetta had carried out her promise to forewarn them of my investigation and it was quickly arranged that I would meet Alfredo at ten o'clock and his sister, Rosina, at ten-thirty next morning, both at the company headquarters in Verona.

On the way out, we looked into the dining room to check what time dinner would be served and Dolores introduced me to Clarissa, the principal, who came as a considerable surprise to me. I had created a mental picture of a grey-haired woman in her sixties with the sort of forbidding facial expression that would have struck fear into the hearts of staff and students alike. Instead, I found myself being introduced to a woman the same sort of age as Dolores and extremely good-looking with it. She had long, dark hair, piled up on her head in a casual but most alluring way, big pendant earrings, and her clothes were unexpected. She had clearly just been playing tennis and her elegant, golden-brown legs reached up to a very short skirt. Instinctively, I stretched out my hand and caught hold of Oscar's collar. His cold, wet nose is drawn to beautiful women in short skirts.

Clarissa gave Anna and me a warm welcome and offered any help she could. I asked if she would mind if I put a few questions to her the following morning and we arranged to meet in her office at nine. Somehow meeting this highly desirable woman who would have been almost exactly the same age as the victim struck me as unexpected and, in consequence, potentially significant. Might there have been something going on between them? Maybe something that had soured so badly that she had resorted to murder?

Still with a wary hand on Oscar's collar, I decided to head off to Verona. Armed with the information that dinner tonight would be served at seven-thirty, we went out to the van.

As an experiment, I reversed out of the parking space slowly so as not to use the brakes and then drove back along the drive to the main gates, which opened automatically. Once again, because of the slight rise in the road, I didn't need to touch the brake pedal and I was able to turn right and start heading downhill towards the scene of the accident still without any use of the brakes. I accelerated hard down the long straight and was doing ninety kilometres per hour before I reached the bend and, no doubt, the E-type would have easily managed to reach an even higher speed.

I slowed when we got to the scene of the accident and pointed out to Anna the scorched tree and the floral tributes. I also underlined to her what I'd just proved to myself. 'It's quite possible that the brakes developed a fault or were tampered with back at the villa and Rodolfo could have been blissfully unaware of the problem until he came down this road at breakneck speed. Certainly, it makes it even more likely that it was brake failure – either accidental or deliberate.'

We followed the road downhill for seven or eight kilometres more until we came to the busy main road that runs around the shores of Lake Garda. I crossed it and set off down a minor road to the lakeside, which was thronged with holidaymakers and their cars. Before setting off, I had checked the location of the café where

Rodolfo might have been heading that day and located it without trouble, relieved to find that it had its own private parking, and I was able to pull in right outside the door. There were tables outside on a terrace close to the water, sheltered by parasols, and we chose one from where we had a fine view over the lake towards the Sirmione promontory with the spectacular Scaligero Castle. This, according to my very own history expert, was built in the thirteenth century and not only had massive defensive walls but also had its own unique fortified harbour surrounded by ramparts. Rising up from the blue waters of the lake, it was an impressive sight.

A few minutes later, a waiter appeared to see what we would like. Anna asked for an ice coffee, and I opted for a cold beer and a bowl of water for Oscar. When the man returned with our drinks, I mentioned Rodolfo's death as casually as possible, and I was surprised to see a look of what might have been disapproval appear on the man's face. Considering the famous singer had supposedly been a customer, I would have expected a degree of regret. I tried giving the waiter a gentle nudge.

'I believe he used to come here for coffee.'

'Every now and then.' Still no friendly reaction from the waiter so I tried again.

'People tell me he was a lovely man. It's such a pity that he died.'

A decidedly sour expression appeared on the man's face but he just mumbled something, picked up his tray and disappeared back through the fly curtain into the café again. I glanced across at Anna. 'That was unexpected.'

She nodded her head and then added, '*Cherchez la femme?* I wonder if the waiter has a wife. Leave it to me; I'll see what I can do.'

With this, she took a small sip of her coffee before getting to her feet and going into the café. She emerged three or four minutes later with a smile on her face.

'This detective business is easy! I got talking to the woman behind the bar and it turns out she's married to Antonio, the waiter. They own the place together. She's probably in her thirties, and when I mentioned the accident, she almost burst into tears. She confirmed that Rodolfo used to drop in from time to time for a coffee and I got the impression that she would have been happy if he'd spent a bit more time with her. Otherwise, she didn't say much – not least because her husband kept coming and going – but it was clear to me that she liked Rodolfo a lot.'

Might this mean that Rodolfo had been involved with this woman as well? If so, might this have provoked the husband to take revenge? We sat and sipped our drinks, savouring the relative cool of the breeze coming off the water, while Oscar stretched out on the ground at our feet. I asked Anna which sights she particularly wanted to see in Verona and it came as no surprise to find that she'd been doing her homework.

'Well, there's the Arena, but we'll actually be going in there on Saturday night so that can wait. Otherwise, seeing as Shakespeare set *Romeo and Juliet* in the city, most people go to see Juliet's house and her tomb, but I'm not bothered. Apart from anything else, Juliet didn't exist – and her "tomb" is empty. There was apparently a legend going back to the thirteenth century that hints at the story but that's all it is: a legend.'

'You aren't a Shakespeare fan, then?'

'Very much the opposite. I love Shakespeare. *Romeo and Juliet* is great – if you like a tale of underage sex that ends in tragedy – but I'm a historian so I prefer facts, and Juliet isn't a fact.'

'Right, no Juliet memorabilia, then. So what do you want to see?'

'As we probably won't have much time this afternoon, let's just have a little walk around the *centro storico* and then tomorrow, I can spend the day browsing the old churches, checking out the *Castelvecchio*, the famous bridges and so on.' She glanced down at Oscar. 'And I can take Oscar for company while you go and do your interviews.'

At the sound of his name, Oscar opened one eye but, seeing as nobody was offering him food, he gave a heartfelt sigh and relapsed into sleep again.

10

WEDNESDAY AFTERNOON

It was just after four-thirty when we got to Maurizio's garage. It was bigger than I'd expected and inside the large hangar, I counted half a dozen splendid old vehicles with mechanics working away on them. Maurizio himself was a bit of a surprise. I had been expecting an elderly man with black fingernails, wearing grease-stained overalls, but in fact, he was quite a bit younger than me, and he was wearing shorts and a clean *Pink Floyd in Verona 1989* T-shirt. I introduced myself and when he heard that Violetta had engaged me to investigate, he agreed to show me the remains of the E-type.

It was still on a trailer at the back of the garage, covered with a tarpaulin. I helped him untie this and together, we pulled it back to reveal a mangled, twisted wreck of burnt, blackened metal. As the farmer had said, it was hard to believe that this had once been a sleek, polished sports car and it was immediately clear that there was no earthly chance of rebuilding it. Fortunately, I couldn't see any remains of the driver, which was a blessing, but it was immediately apparent that the engine, which originally would have sprawled about five feet in length under the beautifully aerodynamic bonnet, now occupied barely half of that size. Everything had been crushed together into an amorphous mass. Even the wheels were twisted and warped as the tyres had burned and there was virtually no trace of the rims, let alone the brake lines. I glanced across at Maurizio and he shook his head sadly.

'At least Rodolfo's death must have been instantaneous. The police said there were no skid marks and they've asked me to double-check if the brakes could have been tampered with. They can't find any proof either way and you can see why. God only knows what's in the midst of all that. The rubber brake lines have melted away completely and there's no way of telling if anybody meddled with them.'

From what I could see, he was patently right. This burnt-out wreck wasn't going to produce any clues. I thanked him and tried a different tack. 'How easy would it have been for somebody to tamper with the brakes?'

'For somebody familiar with vehicles of this age, relatively simple. And you wouldn't need any special tools. A pair of wire snippers or even a sharp knife would be able to do it. Drain out the brake fluid and the brakes just stop working.' He gave me a searching look. 'You think he was murdered, don't you?'

I decided that there was no point in trying to dissimulate. 'Yes, I think I do but I'm struggling to prove it. I don't know how well you knew Rodolfo but, assuming for a moment that he was deliberately targeted, can you think of anybody who might have wanted him dead?'

He took his time before replying and I had a feeling he was debating just how much he should tell me. In the end, he came to a decision. 'Rodolfo was a brilliant singer and a great Italian, as well as being the most generous man I know. The last thing I would ever want to do would be to tarnish his reputation, but, if you want the honest truth, I wouldn't be at all surprised if there was a woman involved one way or another.'

'You knew him well?'

'Pretty well. We shared a love of classic cars and he took me out for lunch or dinner quite a few times. He used to give me and my family free tickets for the opera and every Christmas, he sent me and the team here an amazing hamper of food and wine. One thing that emerged quite clearly, though, the more I got to know him, was that he seemed pathologically incapable of not trying it on with every good-looking woman he met. Believe me, Casanova had nothing on him.'

I nodded. 'Other people have said the same thing to me and, of course, if he was having affairs with other women then that throws up all kinds of jealousy scenarios. I don't suppose you can give me any names, can you?'

He shook his head. 'I didn't know him that well but, like I say, it might be useful for you to follow that line of investigation. Otherwise I can't see any of his family murdering him for money, even though he was immensely rich. His family is one of the wealthiest in Verona, if not Italy. Alessia, his wife, is rich in her own right, so my feeling is that it must have had something to do with an affair of the heart.' He gave me a little grin. 'Or, in his case, probably a part of the body a bit lower down than the heart.'

I thanked him and went back out to the van. After recounting to Anna what I'd been told, I set off again but, before heading for the town centre, I took a detour through the industrial part of the city. I'm sure most visitors to Verona never venture out into the suburbs of the city, but Verona is an important commercial hub and it was here that I found the centre of operations of the Agri Argento company. The complex of at least four massive ware-houses occupied several acres behind a security fence and it looked from the gates as though the main admin building had only recently been built. This was a six-storey symphony of plate glass, concrete and steel, and the name of the company stood out against the blue of the sky on the roof of the building in six-foot-high white letters, vaguely reminiscent of the Hollywood sign. Nobody could be in any doubt that this company was a major player.

Now that I knew where my meetings were going to take place the following morning, I didn't bother stopping, and we headed back towards the *centro storico*. Finding a parking space took quite a while and it was with considerable relief that I finally managed to slip into a slot recently vacated by a Dutch-registered camper van. This was a short walk from the main avenue leading up from the station and we entered the *centro storico* through the ancient stone double arch in the city walls beyond which we could see the huge bulk of the Arena. We walked into Piazza Bra that, ironically, has a lingerie shop on the corner – well, it made me laugh even if Anna smiled dutifully but didn't appear to share the joke. All along the left-hand side of the wide piazza were bars and restaurants getting ready for the arrival of hungry tourists, and the whole place was humming with a multilingual mix of humanity.

Towering over all the surrounding buildings was the impressive circular mass of the Arena with its row upon row of stone arches. It was easy to imagine crowds of Roman citizens queuing up to join twenty or thirty thousand of their fellow countrymen and women as they watched gladiators slaughtering each other or wild animals devouring hapless prisoners for the delight of the mob. It was a relief to know that this stadium was now used for far less bloodthirsty pursuits – like opera and, indeed, a number of pop concerts like the famous Pink Floyd concert featured on Maurizio's T-shirt.

We made our way along what looked like one of the main shopping streets where designer boutiques offered luxury goods at terrifying prices. I kept a watchful eye on Oscar's nose amid the crowds to avoid him getting too familiar with the tourists, for the most part dressed in short skirts and shorts. Thankfully, he behaved himself and I was able to relax. Even though it was evening by now, the sun was still hot, but here in the shade of the buildings lining the street, the temperature was just about acceptable.

After walking for about half an hour, dodging the crowds and the never-ending stream of battered old bikes that shared the pedestrian area with the tourists, I checked my watch and turned to Anna.

'Time to head back. We don't want to be late for dinner.'

Oscar looked up, nodded, and immediately set off in the direction of the van. When it comes to his food, his comprehension skills are second to none.

I was secretly relieved to find that the other residents of the villa were no longer sporting opera costumes. It was seven-fifteen when we went downstairs and we found at least a dozen people standing around in the bar area chatting while they waited for dinner. I went over and ordered a glass of white wine for Anna and a cold beer for myself and was pleasantly surprised to find that I wasn't charged anything. The waiter at the bar shook his head as he handed me the drinks.

'You are Signora Violetta's guests. She was most insistent that you should have free access to everything.'

I thanked him warmly and took the drinks across to Anna, who had struck up a conversation with a pair of middle-aged women who were presumably part of the teaching staff. She hastened to introduce them to me and we shook hands. Although the names meant nothing to me, it was clear that these two had been performers in their time – and, indeed, maybe still were – and Anna had recognised their faces and maybe even remembered their names. I joined the conversation and gently brought it around to the death of the founder of the academy. I was fascinated to see their expressions change when Rodolfo was mentioned. The taller of the two shook her head sadly while a distinct expression of disapproval appeared on the other woman's face. Gradually, doing my best not to sound too obvious, I managed to get them to give me their personal opinions of the victim.

The taller woman, Maria Something-or-other, looked genuinely upset at Rodolfo's death and she was quick to praise him for his amazing generosity in setting up the academy and sponsoring so many young people. Her companion, Silvia, took a bit of persuading but, in the end, I managed to get her talking. What she had to say was fascinating.

'Rodolfo was a complex character. Yes, he was immensely generous and all the students here have good reason to be very grateful to him, but, at the same time, he had a predatory streak.'

'Predatory in what way?' I tried to sound just mildly interested although I was pretty sure I knew what was coming.

'Rodolfo was a sex pest.'

Maria immediately objected. 'That's unfair, Silvia. Yes, he was a flirt but he never imposed himself on anybody. Any woman who decided to take up with him did so willingly. There was no question of coercion.'

Silvia didn't look convinced. 'I'm not so sure. I think a number of women here felt they had to go along with his advances just to show their gratitude. I find that rather distasteful.'

This appeared to confirm what Dolores had told me and I filed it away for further study. I could well imagine how any woman might feel if she had been pressurised into having sex with a man in this way. Maybe angry enough to commit murder?

Any further conversation was interrupted by the sound of the gong and we all made our way into the dining room. Maria and Silvia disappeared off to another table and Anna and I sat down by ourselves. A few minutes later, we were joined by another couple. I didn't recognise the woman but I immediately recognised the man. This was Romeo, the Don Juan of the academy. He gave Anna a broad smile and introduced himself and his partner. 'It's good to see new faces. My name's Romeo and this is my cousin, Veronica.'

He was probably in his early thirties and his cousin maybe a year or two older. What rapidly became clear, however, was that Romeo almost completely ignored his cousin. Instead, I could see that he was definitely enjoying sitting next to Anna – in spite of her being fifteen or twenty years older than him – and it didn't take long before he was starting to get on my nerves with his constant banter, accompanied by regular touches of her hand and arm. I was just toying with the idea of trying to persuade Oscar to go around to tear him limb from limb – some hopes unless he had a pork chop in his pocket – when Anna took direct action. Totally ignoring Romeo, she leant across him and spoke directly to Veronica.

'Does your cousin have an on/off switch? His constant flirting soon gets on your nerves, doesn't it?'

An expression of hurt pride appeared on Romeo's face and I had to struggle to restrain a smile. Veronica replied with a grin. 'You have to admire his self-confidence, but I know what you mean.' She looked up at the now red-faced man. 'Romeo, just for once, could you try to forget that you think you're the greatest lover who ever lived?'

This was the perfect intro for me. 'I thought that position was reserved for Rodolfo Argento. From what people have been saying, it seems that he thought *he* was the reincarnation of Casanova.'

The expression on Romeo's face changed from annoyance – and no little degree of embarrassment – to clear animosity. 'Rodolfo was totally up himself. What woman could possibly be interested in a narcissist like him?'

Veronica gave him her sweetest smile. 'It's amazing how many narcissists there are about – some really close at hand.'

Clearly, by this time, Romeo had had enough and he jumped to his feet. Oscar looked up in surprise as the man gave us a peremptory nod of the head. 'If you'll excuse me, there's some-body over there I need to see.' And he headed off across the room. As he did so, Anna and Veronica dissolved into fits of giggles and I reached over to grasp Anna's hand on the tabletop.

'Poor guy, he'll probably never flirt with another woman again.'

Veronica shook her head. 'Water off a duck's back to Romeo. Look at him now.'

Sure enough, the reincarnation of Casanova had settled down on a table with two women and was soon chatting them up assiduously. Veronica stood up and excused herself. 'I might need to rescue those two before long, so I'd better go. *Buon appetito.*'

As she walked off, any further consideration of Romeo was interrupted by the arrival of a new face.

'Mr Armstrong? I wonder if I could join you.' The new arrival was a very attractive woman and I had already worked out who she was by the time she introduced herself. 'I'm Alessia Ricco, Rodolfo's wife... widow.'

11

WEDNESDAY EVENING

Alessia came across as charming. She told us she had spent the last few days performing in Naples and Salerno and had driven back this afternoon in her beloved old Porsche. She smiled a lot and projected a friendly personality, although it appeared to be an effort. The impression she gave was that she was still grieving for her husband but, of course, that might have been an act. My ex-wife often accused me of being too cynical, but a lifetime in the murder squad had made me loath to take any possible suspect at face value. Nevertheless, when Anna and I offered our condolences, a shadow passed over the widow's face and her eyes dropped. If it was an act, it was a good one.

'I still can't believe he's gone. It seems only yesterday he was telling me about his plans for the next few months.' Her voice broke as she spoke and I gave her a few moments before continuing with the enquiry, keeping my tone low and respectful.

'I understand he'd just been told that he would be singing in Venice at Christmas in front of some very illustrious company.'

'Yes, he was very excited about that.' She produced a tissue and wiped real tears from her eyes. As any actor will tell you, that takes a bit of doing so, I told myself, maybe she was genuinely grieving. Still, I couldn't help querying what she had been doing since his death.

'And you've been performing, so soon after his death? Couldn't you have got out of it?'

'My agent was all for cancelling my tour but, to be honest, performing takes my mind off things, so I was determined to carry on with the commitments rather than just mope around here on my own.' She looked up and the pain in her eyes looked genuine to me. 'It was just at night, alone in the hotel, that it was tough.'

I decided not to mention my reason for being here, but the grieving widow's mind was clearly working along the same lines as my own. She looked me straight in the eye and spoke in measured, serious tones. 'The police had a theory that Rodolfo might have tried to kill himself. That's rubbish. Life was good for him. There's no question about that.'

'So if it wasn't suicide, the only viable explanation is brake failure. Do you think that's a possibility?'

She shook her head decisively. 'Out of the question. That car was in perfect condition – I used to drive it myself whenever I could and it ran like clockwork. He was always working on it and there's no way he could have overlooked something as serious as a problem with the brakes.'

I didn't add the obvious conclusion that the car might have been tampered with. Instead, I let Anna steer the conversation back to music and we settled down to eat. Dinner was every bit as good as lunch. It started with some excellent cured ham and salami accompanied by fresh figs, and this was followed by a ham and mushroom risotto. The main course was a tasty chicken stew and I was amazed that my fellow diners weren't all grossly overweight if they ate two meals like this every day. Presumably, their lessons kept them busy, the tennis courts kept them fit, and quite probably a certain amount of extra-curricular hanky-panky helped to burn off a few calories. The wine was as good as ever, although Anna and Alessia stuck to mineral water. After an excellent crème caramel, I decided to lay my cards on the table for her.

'I don't know if you've heard from Violetta, but she's asked me to come up here and look into what might have been the real cause of your husband's death – I'm a private investigator based in Florence. She's convinced that his death was no accident and that somebody must have deliberately tampered with the Jaguar's brakes. To that end, I wonder if you'd be able to give me a few minutes of your time. I really need to know as much as I can about Rodolfo.'

I had been keeping a careful eye on the widow as I explained what I was doing here and I observed the very positive way she reacted. 'No, Violetta hasn't said anything and it was Dolores who just told me now that you and Anna might be interesting to talk to – although she didn't go into any detail. I'm very pleased to know that's why you're here because I totally agree with Violetta – not something I do very often. He was murdered; I have no doubt about that. Any help I can give to find the person who robbed me of the love of my life, just ask.'

I gave her a little smile, once again impressed at her apparent sincerity. 'Thank you, that's excellent. Are you happy to have that conversation now or would you prefer to get a good night's sleep first? You have had a long drive, after all.'

'I'm fine and I'm more than happy to talk to you now. Would you like a coffee first?'

After ordering coffees, I pulled out my notebook and embarked on a series of questions.

'I couldn't help noticing that you said you don't often see eye to eye with Violetta. Could you tell me how you would categorise your relationship with your mother-in-law?'

She hesitated for a few moments. 'I think "strained" would be the polite way of putting it. She and Rodolfo had a strange relationship – to my mind not a very healthy one. It was clear that she worshipped the ground he walked on and it was equally clear that she could do no wrong in his eyes.' She looked across the table and gave me a weak smile. 'You can probably imagine how difficult it was for me in the middle of that.'

I certainly could. I had already gained the impression that Violetta's relationship with her son had been very close and I could sympathise with the new wife caught up in the middle of some fairly tight apron strings. Whether that could have led to such frustration that murder had appeared the best solution remained to be seen. I left that subject for now and stuck to generalities.

'You were married last September?'

She nodded.

'How would you describe your relationship with your husband?'

She didn't hesitate. 'Warm, loving, trusting.'

'I'm interested that you use the word "trusting". A lot of the people I've been speaking to seem to think that your husband was an inveterate womaniser. What do you say to them?'

Her expression soured. 'I would tell them to mind their own business. Of course I knew when I met Rodolfo that he had a reputation, but I can honestly say that, since getting married, I have absolutely no doubt that he was ever unfaithful to me once. Nor I to him.'

This last remark was in stark contrast to the allegations

levelled against her by Violetta, but I decided not to rake them up for now. After all, Dolores had had no doubts about Alessia's probity, so maybe this was all the work of the octogenarian's malicious imagination.

'If we consider for a moment that your husband might have been murdered, can you think of any enemies he might have had? Is there anybody who stood to win or lose as a result of his death?'

'I suppose the only winner is Violetta, who's inherited half of his considerable wealth – much to the chagrin of his cousins, I'm sure, but I can't see a mother murdering her son, can you? In an opera maybe, but not in real life. Not least a mother who so clearly doted on her son and he on her. Their relationship was so close, I felt almost jealous sometimes.' She deliberately looked me straight in the eye. 'And of course the other person to benefit is me. I'm many millions of euros richer than I was before his death, but I would give it all away in an instant just to have him here with me.' I couldn't miss the tears back in her eyes and I couldn't detect any hint of insincerity in her voice. If it was a performance, it was a very convincing one. Interestingly, this provoked a movement from under the table and Oscar emerged, stretched, and wandered over to Alessia's side, where he sat down and laid a heavy black paw on her knee in a sign of solidarity. He always seems to know when somebody needs the canine equivalent of a hug. She smiled at him and fondled his ears.

I carried on with my questions. 'How do you get on with Rodolfo's cousins? Do you see much of them?'

She paused for a few seconds' reflection. 'I like Rosina and I think she likes me. I see her every now and then. Her brother, Alfredo, keeps himself to himself and I rarely speak to him or Ingrid, his wife. I'm afraid I've never really got on with her. I think she made up her mind at an early stage that I was just a gold-digger and she's never been able to give me the benefit of the doubt.'

'And Violetta? She's a very self-opinionated old lady. How difficult were things between the two of you?'

Alessia shook her head sadly. 'It's a shame. I'm sure I could really have got to like her if it hadn't been for her suffocating influence on her son. She has so much character, but I'm afraid her opinion of me is probably the same as Ingrid's.'

'She thinks you're a gold-digger?'

'I'm not sure if she thought I was after his money, but she and I have never seen eye to eye. Like I told you, her relationship with Rodolfo was intense and I suppose no woman was ever going to match up to her expectations for her beloved son.'

'Can you think of anybody outside the family who might have wished harm to your husband?'

'A few years ago, quite possibly. Like I told you, I knew his reputation and it wasn't pretty. I'm sure there were numerous cuckolded husbands and discarded lovers with a burning hatred of him, but that was before I came along. He was still a terrible flirt after I met him, but it no longer led anywhere. I can genuinely confirm that what we had was real love and I trusted him implicitly.'

After this unswerving vote of confidence I saw little point in continuing the questioning. Unless Alessia was a remarkably good actress, it seemed clear that she utterly denied the accusations I had been hearing – and Oscar appeared convinced of her sincerity. If her assertion that her husband had changed his ways was indeed the truth, then it neatly removed a whole heap of jilted lovers and brought me back to his immediate family. Still, even if it was just for the record, there was one question I knew I had to ask.

'Would you mind telling me where you were on the day of the accident? I'm asking everybody.' Even though I wasn't.

'I was here with Rodolfo. At least, we were here for part of the morning but then we both went down to the Porsche dealer in Verona to pick up a new tailpipe and a few other bits for my car. We were probably away for an hour or so.'

'And that was in your Porsche?'

'That's correct, yes.'

'And for the rest of the morning?'

'We were together. We went upstairs but then came down for lunch in the dining room with the other residents. I was only really separated from him when he went off after lunch and of course then...' Her voice tailed off.

'I believe I heard that he was going down to the lake for a walk. I'm surprised you didn't go with him. Why was that?'

'He was upset. Not with me but with one of the students who annoyed him.'

'Really? I thought everybody here loved him.'

'Most of them did but not all...' There was a pause before she carried on. 'To tell the truth, one of the students made a comment about my dress and Rodolfo took exception to what he said.'

'What did the student say?'

'I can't remember the exact words but he was commenting on my cleavage. It was a hot day and I was wearing a very loose blouse – but I certainly wasn't indecent.'

'Can you remember the name of the student?' I had a premonition that I would recognise the name when I heard it – and I was right.

'He's a man called Romeo. He's okay but he's just a bit too full of himself. You know the type – he reckons he's God's gift to women. Anyway, Rodolfo sent him off with a flea in his ear, but it put him in a bad mood so he told me he was going off to clear his head. I remember asking him to make sure he brought the car back before half past two as I needed it to go down to the hairdressers in Verona for a three o'clock appointment. I couldn't drive my Porsche as it was making a terrible racket.' She looked up at me. 'That was the last thing I ever said to him.' There was a catch in her voice and I gave her a minute to collect herself before I carried on with the questions.

'And while you went into Verona that morning to buy the new exhaust for your vehicle, was the garage here locked or open?'

'Definitely locked. I don't think he went into the garage that morning. My car was parked outside the main entrance. The idea was to put it up on the ramp next morning and fix the exhaust.'

A thought occurred to me, and I changed the subject. 'Do you know your husband's agent...' I consulted my notepad, '...Paolo Ruggieri? Can you tell me anything about him?'

She shrugged. 'What can I say? Paolo's an agent, and we all know what they're like.'

I shook my head. 'I'm sorry, but I have limited experience of theatrical agents. What are they like?'

She even managed a little grin. 'Devious, honey-tongued and only too happy to promise the earth.'

'And did he deliver the goods? Was he an effective agent?'

'Yes, I suppose so, but you could argue that it was Rodolfo's reputation that made things so easy for Paolo.'

'Did you ever hear your husband complain about him? Was there ever any bad blood between them?'

'Rodolfo sometimes moaned about the fact that Paolo did very little, but I never heard them argue seriously.' She paused for thought. 'Apart from just a few days before the accident. They had a major argument on the phone. I didn't hear what it was all about, but it was clear that Rodolfo was furious about something that Paolo had said.'

'And you can't remember what the argument was about?'

She shook her head. 'No, when the call finished, I asked

Rodolfo, but he was so angry, he just went out to his car and drove down to the lake again. That's what he did when he was upset. He would park by Antonio's café down there, walk along the lakeside until he calmed down and then he'd stop off for a coffee on his way back. According to Rodolfo, they make the best coffee in the area. By the time he came back again an hour after the argument with Paolo, he had settled down and when I asked him what it had been about, he just said, "Business." I didn't ask him again.'

'I don't suppose you have a contact number for Paolo Ruggieri, have you?'

She pulled out her phone and gave me the number. I thanked her very much for her help and we chatted a bit longer before she bade us goodnight and went off to her apartment.

After she'd left, I looked across at Anna. 'What did you think of the mourning widow?'

'I liked her and I definitely got the impression she loved her husband deeply. I'd be amazed if she were involved in his death. When you told her why you were here, she looked genuinely pleased. What about you? Did she make the same impression on you?'

'To be honest, yes. Of course, she's used to performing on stage so she might have been acting, but it was a very convincing act. I'm interested in what she said about the argument her husband had with his agent, only days before his death. I'd love to know what that was about and he's going on my list of people I need to interview.'

Before I could say any more, there was the sound of a chair being pushed back and a young man, probably just into his twenties, stood up and launched into song. He had a fine voice and he sang for about three or four minutes, interestingly accompanied by about half the room by the end – mercifully not including

Oscar. When they stopped, I joined in the applause before returning my attention to Anna.

'The spirit of Verdi Wednesday lives on. Was that a piece by Verdi as well? I recognised the tune, even if I couldn't make head or tail of the words.'

She beamed at me. 'We'll make an opera connoisseur out of you yet, Dan. That was probably one of the most famous pieces of opera in the world – "La donna è mobile" – and, yes, it's by Verdi. It comes from Rigoletto and it's sung by the Duke of Mantua. That young tenor has a fine voice.' Her expression became more serious. 'So you don't think Alessia did it?'

'Anything's possible but, like I said, I tended to believe her and I definitely got the feeling she was a loving wife.' I glanced down at my feet and saw Oscar surveying me closely. 'And Oscar reckoned she was on the level as well. Yes, dog, you need your evening stroll, don't you?' I returned my attention to Anna. 'Feel like coming with me?'

Anna shook her head. 'To be quite honest, I don't really. I'm absolutely full after that meal and all I want to do is go and sit down quietly and watch the news while I summon up the energy to take a shower and go to bed.'

I glanced down at Oscar. 'Looks like it's just you and me, buddy, or shall we see if your girlfriend wants to come with us?'

I swear he nodded.

I checked with the waitress, who explained to me where Dolores had her apartment, and I easily located this at the rear of the villa near the kitchens. I tapped on the door and Dolores appeared almost immediately with Elektra at her side. Oscar's tail immediately started wagging furiously.

'Hi, Dolores, I'm just taking Oscar for a walk and I wondered if you wanted me to take Elektra as well?'

She smiled gratefully. 'That would be terrific, thanks.'

I was just turning to leave with the two Labradors when a thought occurred to me. 'I'm trying to work out exactly who had access to the keys to the garage. Am I right in thinking there was only Rodolfo, Alessia, Beppe and maybe Violetta? Anybody else you can think of?'

She shook her head. 'No, just the four of them – and my master key in the safe to which Clarissa and I both have access, not that we ever use it. Of course, Rodolfo's key was lost in the accident along with all his possessions, but if you want to get into the garage, I can give you the master key if you want it. Would you like it?'

'Thank you, that could be very useful.'

She quickly retrieved the remote control from the safe and I slipped it into my pocket before going out into the night accompanied by the two happy Labradors. It was just after nine and, although the sun had disappeared behind the mountains, there was still light in the sky and it was easy to see where we were going. I headed back along the drive towards the main gate, stopping off in the big field to let the dogs have a run around. Oscar wasted no time in finding a huge pine cone, which I kicked around for him to retrieve while Elektra looked on in bewilderment. Clearly, she hadn't inherited the Labrador retriever gene the same way as Oscar.

It was a delightful evening and as I wandered around, I realised that I was humming to myself and I was impressed to note that it was none other than 'La donna è mobile'. As I hummed 'dum-dum-dum-diddly-dum', I reflected that there was maybe something to this opera business after all – either that or I was being brainwashed.

After a half-hour walk in the pleasantly cooler evening air, we returned to the villa and I remembered the remote control in my pocket. Heading around to the side of the villa, I opened the garage door and switched on the lights to reveal the lovely old cars.

While Elektra wandered around sniffing, I kept a careful eye on Oscar in case he decided to start peeing on the tyres, but he seemed more interested in his female companion. I also did a bit of sniffing around. I started with the spot where the Jaguar had lived before the accident. I wasn't really sure what I was looking for, although a pool of brake fluid on the floor would have been handy, but I saw little of interest. In fact, if anything, it looked as though somebody had even run a mop over the space, as it was remarkably clean. Needless to say, to my suspicious mind, this raised a number of questions. Who had cleaned the floor and why? Had this been simply a matter of tidying up or had it been designed to remove potentially incriminating evidence?

I followed the dogs down between the cars until I reached the workbench. On top of this were a number of tools with a whole rack of others hanging on the wall behind it. At the foot of the bench was a fire extinguisher and a rubbish bin, mostly containing empty motor-oil containers. Out of idle curiosity, I flicked through them with my fingers until I came to one that was clearly still full. This was unexpected so I removed a tissue from my pocket, used it as I pulled the container out and unscrewed the top. I may not be the world's best mechanic but I am familiar with the smell of brake fluid and my nose immediately identified the contents of the container, in spite of it being marked *20W50 Motor Oil*. I set the can down on the workbench and stared at it. Did this contain the brake fluid from the Jaguar that somebody had removed? Was this the proof that his crash had been no accident?

I opened a cupboard door and managed to make a space at the back of a shelf where I could put this container before hiding it behind a barrier of other bits and pieces. I felt sure it would be safe here and there would be no question of Beppe throwing it out with the rubbish. I closed the cupboard door and looked down at Oscar.

'Wouldn't it be nice if there was a nice set of fingerprints on that container?'

Glad to be included in the conversation, he looked for a moment as though he nodded, before returning his attention to his new girlfriend.

12

THURSDAY MORNING

Next morning dawned bright and clear once again. Anna was still asleep and as it was early, I didn't disturb Dolores to see whether Elektra wanted to join us, so Oscar and I went for a walk by ourselves. The temperature was delightful and we had an excellent walk down through the vineyards and back up again, passing by the copse of trees where, needless to say, Oscar found a suitable selection of sticks to retrieve.

While I watched him having a good time, I considered what my course of action for today should be. I felt confident that the brake fluid I had located the previous night was likely to prove significant in the investigation and I knew that I would have to speak to the police sooner rather than later. At nine o'clock, I was scheduled to meet up with Clarissa, the principal, and then at ten o'clock, I would have the first of my appointments with Rodolfo's cousins. I decided to go through with these before going to the police. I was tempted for a moment to call Virgilio, my newly promoted *commissario* friend in Florence, to ask whether he knew anybody in the Verona force, but on reflection, I decided to leave him in peace. Hopefully, the officers here would accept my input as cooperation rather than interference.

It came as no surprise to find the dining room only half full at breakfast time. Italians don't normally get excited about breakfast the way we Brits do. A quick coffee and a croissant are all that most opt for. I was therefore delighted to find not only fresh fruit salad and a choice of breads, jams and cakes but also slices of cheese and ham and even the offer of fried eggs or an omelette, which I declined. While Anna sipped her café latte and nibbled a croissant, I made myself a ham and cheese sandwich and followed it with a couple of buns. I had a feeling that my visit to the police later this morning might well develop into something time-consuming so I had no idea when my next meal would be coming. At least, that was the way I justified it to myself.

At nine o'clock, I made my way to the office of the principal and tapped on the door. A voice told me to enter and I found Clarissa sitting, not behind her desk, but on one of a pair of armchairs by a coffee table. She was no longer wearing her tennis kit but was elegantly dressed, her hair perfect. I kept Oscar at my side just in case he might decide to get too friendly and try to climb onto her lap – it has happened before.

She gave him a warm smile. 'What a lovely dog. I thought it was Elektra for a moment but this one has much more expressive eyes. What's his name?'

'He's Oscar.' I sat down opposite Clarissa and pulled out my notebook. 'I just wanted to ask you a few quick questions, if you don't mind. The first one I'm obliged to ask everybody: where were you on the day of the accident?'

'Here in my office, working.' She consulted her phone. 'Apart from eleven until twelve when I was sitting in on a rehearsal for our Midsummer Concert – that's coming up tomorrow night. We do it every year but this year, as you can imagine, it's going to be specially for Rodolfo. I do hope you'll be able to attend.'

'That sounds wonderful. I'll tell Anna. I'm sure she'll be very excited.' I avoided rolling my eyes. This meant I was going to have a double helping of opera. Somehow, I had a feeling I would emerge from this week in Verona either as a convinced opera fan or the opposite. Time would tell. Returning to my questions, I did a bit of double-checking. 'Can anybody confirm that you were in your office the rest of the time, particularly in the morning?' I gave her my usual apologetic look. 'Like I say, I'm asking everybody the same thing.'

'I quite understand. No, I was on my own – apart from lunchtime, when I was in the dining room with everybody. I made a few phone calls to people so I expect if you want to check the phone records, that might provide something.' She sounded quite genuine so I didn't pursue it further for the moment.

'How long have you worked here?'

'Two and a half years. I used to be at La Scala in Milan.'

'Another question I'm asking everybody: can you think of anybody who would have wanted to harm or kill Rodolfo Argento?'

'No, I can't.' Her answer came back immediately. 'Particularly here, he was almost revered. You can ask any of the students or staff. They loved him, as did I.'

There was something almost wistful in her final words and my suspicion that there might have been something going on between her and the victim increased.

'When you say that everybody loved him, I've been hearing stories that maybe some of the women took that to extremes.'

'People say such terrible things about him, but they're wrong.' There was a note of real regret in her voice. 'He was a beautiful man, such a talented man and, oh so generous. I do wish these people who spread malicious rumours would stop. Yes, I know he had a poor reputation in the past, but I can tell you most clearly that in all the time I knew him, he always behaved like a perfect gentleman.'

'I've been told that ever since he got married last autumn, he was a changed man. Would you agree with that?'

'I would certainly agree that he and Alessia seemed to have a solid relationship. I'm sure he believed he loved her very dearly.' I couldn't miss the vague way she had phrased her answers. Hardly a ringing endorsement. I found myself wondering whether Clarissa might have wished for a closer relationship with her boss. Had she maybe even hooked up with him only to find herself discarded in favour of his new wife? What was that old expression about hell having no fury?

By the time I finished interviewing her, I had added her to my list of possibles, although I had to admit that she had answered my questions willingly and apparently sincerely. I applied the MOM test to her, as I had been taught many years ago. The acronym stood for motive, opportunity and means. Jealousy might have provided her with a motive, she had access to the garage key in the safe so she had opportunity but, as far as I could tell, she lacked the means. She would appear to have no experience of car mechanics, which would make it less likely – but not impossible – that she would have known how to tamper with the brakes of the Jaguar.

I collected Anna, went over to the garage, slipped the oil container into a clean plastic bag, and stowed it carefully in the van before driving down to Verona. I dropped Anna and Oscar off at the entrance to Piazza Bra, promising to call her when my interviews had finished. From there, I drove back to the Agri Argento site and rolled up to the barrier at the main gate. A burly man in uniform came out of a cabin and I explained who I was and why I was here. After consulting a clipboard and speaking on the phone, he waved me through and indicated that I should park alongside a lurid-green supercar – presumably Alfredo's new Lamborghini. 'Go up the steps to the main entrance and somebody will meet you in the lobby and accompany you to the top floor. Have a nice day, sir.'

I did as instructed and found a smart young man waiting in the large, marble-clad lobby. He came forward and held out his hand. 'Mr Armstrong, good morning. My name is Matteo. If you'd like to follow me...'

He spoke to me in good English and he and I had a little chat in the lift as it hummed up to the sixth floor. He told me he had worked for the company for seven years and sounded as though he enjoyed his work. When we reached the top floor, he handed me over to a young woman sitting behind a glass desk directly opposite the lift. She looked up at me over the rims of her glasses.

'Signor Armstrong, if you'd like to take a seat, I'll tell Signor Alfredo that you've arrived.' Unlike the young man, she addressed me in Italian, and I recognised her voice from our brief telephone conversation the previous day when I had made the appointments. She picked up the phone and I had barely sat down when one of the doors behind her opened and an auburn-haired man appeared. He looked about forty or so, suntanned and fit, and he was wearing a light-blue polo shirt with *Verona Golf and Country Club* on his left breast. Clearly, this was Alfredo. He strode across to greet me, hand extended.

'Signor Armstrong, I'm very pleased to meet you. Do come in.'

He waved me into his office, which was very much as I'd been expecting: large, luxurious and imposing. There was a closed laptop on his desk but otherwise there was remarkably little clutter. Ignoring the businesslike conference table and chairs, he led

me across to a fine pair of leather sofas by one of the big windows
and indicated that I should sit down.

'Can I offer you anything? A coffee maybe?'

I thanked him and declined, waiting until he had sat down
opposite me before launching into my story. I told him how I'd
been approached by Violetta to investigate the circumstances of
her son's death and asked him if he minded answering a few questions. He gave me a broad smile and sat back in preparation,
although to an old cynic like me, that gave the impression he was
maybe trying a bit too hard to be affable. 'Fire away. Any help I can
give, I'll be only too happy.'

'Thank you, Signor Argento. I've been asking everybody this,
but can you tell me whether Rodolfo might have had any
enemies?'

His expression became more serious. 'You seriously think it
might not have been an accident?'

'I'm afraid so. It's looking increasingly as though the brakes of
his Jaguar might have been tampered with.'

He looked genuinely appalled. 'Really? But who could have
done such a thing?'

'That's what I'm trying to establish. I ask again, did your cousin
have any enemies?'

He shook his head. 'Very much the opposite; he was widely
loved and respected.' He paused before qualifying his statement.
'A few years ago, I dare say there would have been any number of
unhappy women he had wronged or their partners out for his
blood, but not now. Although I confess that I don't have a lot of
time for Alessia, since they married last year, I very much got the
impression that Rodolfo had finally become more settled.' He
looked up from his hands. 'So, I honestly can't think of anybody
who might have been his enemy and certainly nobody who could
possibly have considered committing murder.'

'Might there be any other reason for somebody to want him dead? I'm sorry to have to ask you this, but I understand from Violetta that he was a very wealthy man and a number of people stood to inherit considerable sums of money upon his death.'

He looked up at me in disbelief. 'Are you trying to say that somebody in the family might have killed him? I'm sorry but I won't dignify that with a reply. It's absolutely beyond belief.' He sounded genuinely outraged and I found myself tending to believe him. Nevertheless, I tried one more little push.

'Not necessarily in the family. I understand that his agent inherited a million euros. That's not an insignificant sum.'

'Ruggieri a murderer?' He scoffed. 'I question whether he could bring himself to kill a fly and if, as you say, the murderer tampered with the brakes of Rodolfo's car, then you can definitely exclude Paolo Ruggieri. I've never met anybody less practical. I had to help him take the top off his pen last time I saw him.' And this coming from the man Beppe had described as severely impractical himself.

'I understand that, according to the terms of the will, it's now Violetta who takes over Rodolfo's share. Is that going to be a problem for you and your sister?'

To my surprise, he smiled. 'I'll know more tomorrow. We have a board meeting at three and Violetta will be there. I'm sure we'll be discussing the structure of the company in the wake of Rodolfo's death. I can't see how it will change very much. She's always been pretty hands-on.'

We continued chatting but it soon became clear that there was little more he could offer me – apart from a glowing review of the local golf course. By the time ten-thirty came around, I had learned nothing that advanced my enquiries but I had to admit, albeit grudgingly, that I tended to think that it was unlikely that he'd had anything to do with his cousin's death. We shook hands and he repeated his willingness to offer any help he could before leading me out and handing me over to the woman at the glass desk. She immediately picked up the phone. 'I'll call Signora Rosina.'

While I sat and waited, I reflected on the conversation I had just had with her boss. The one question I would have liked to put to him, but I'd felt sure would have led to an eruption of indignation, would have been to ask about his wife's relations with the dead man. According to Violetta, she had been furious when she had heard the terms of the will. How had relations been between her and Rodolfo before the singer's death? I decided that I would try to find answers to these questions when I spoke to Alfredo's sister. At that moment, the woman herself emerged from a door a bit further along from where I was sitting.

'Signor Armstrong, I gather you're here to help. Do come in.' We shook hands and I followed her into her office. With her auburn hair, the resemblance to her brother was immediately evident, and her office was a carbon copy of her brother's, but with one major difference. Almost every horizontal surface here appeared to be covered with files and papers. There were no fewer than three computers on or near her desk and the contrast with the barren nature of her brother's office was striking. Violetta appeared to have been right – it certainly looked as though Rosina did the lion's share of the work around here. She sat down at her desk and waved me into a seat opposite her. She was a friendly looking woman, probably fifteen years younger than me, and I felt sure Oscar would have given her his seal of approval. She didn't waste time with small talk.

'I understand from Violetta that you and she believe that Rodolfo was murdered. Can you prove that?'

I nodded slowly. 'I believe I might be able to now. Once I've finished my interviews with you and your brother, my next destination is the police station to pass on to them what I've uncovered. I'm afraid it could well be that your cousin was murdered.'

She looked shocked, but not excessively so. Certainly, in comparison to her brother, it appeared to have come as less of a surprise to her. 'And do you have any idea who might have done it?'

I shook my head. 'For now, nothing, but the police might be able to discover some clues when I pass on the information I have to them. Can you think of anybody who would have wished to harm your cousin?'

She then told me pretty much the same as the others had about him having been a womaniser in the past but she, like her brother, indicated that she felt sure he had calmed down since last autumn. 'Marrying Alessia was the very best thing that could have happened to him. She finally managed to get him to settle down and we were all very relieved about that.'

'Tell me about Alessia. Do you and she get on well together?'

She nodded. 'Yes, I have a lot of time for her. She works hard, she's very talented and she's done well for herself. I also believe she genuinely loved Rodolfo. I know Violetta and Ingrid didn't approve of her, but I think that's more a reflection on their lack of tolerance than on Alessia.'

'So you can't imagine her having been involved in her husband's death?'

'Good Lord above, no. Absolutely not. Like I told you, she genuinely loved him and he loved her. I'm quite sure of that.' Yet another person contradicting what Violetta had told me. It certainly sounded as if it had been a match made in heaven – to all but the mother-in-law. 'You mentioned your sister-in-law, Ingrid, and that relations between her and Alessia might not have been that close. Can you tell me a bit more?'

'Ingrid made no secret of the fact that she believed Alessia had only got together with Rodolfo for his money. This is patently ridiculous because Alessia is very well off in her own right and, besides, it was perfectly clear to me and to most people that it was a love match between them.'

'So why do you think Ingrid was so hard on her?'

Rosina's answer raised my eyebrows.

'Can I tell you something in confidence, Mr Armstrong?' I nodded and she continued. 'Strictly between the two of us, and I mean just the two of us, I think it takes one to know one.'

'You're saying that you think Ingrid married your brother for his money?' Could it be that Rodolfo's success had made Ingrid begin to think she might have married the wrong cousin? The ramifications of this were fascinating and I listened attentively to what Rosina had to say about her sister-in-law.

'I've always thought that. All right, they've been married now for ten years and I suppose if she had just been into Alfredo for his money, she could have divorced him by now, but I have little doubt that his wealth was the main stimulus driving her when she first met and then married him. Have you met her?'

'Not yet.'

'Well, you'll see that she's a very beautiful woman, and she's always known it. Ten years ago, she played the field until she found herself her very own millionaire.'

My mind was racing. Might the beautiful Ingrid have developed an illicit relationship with her husband's womanising cousin? Had that ended with the arrival of Alessia and might this have stirred her into an outburst of jealous rage? I tried to dig a bit deeper into Ingrid's relationship with her husband. 'Would you say that she and your brother have a happy marriage?'

She shrugged. 'I suppose so, although I know he would have wanted children.'

'And Ingrid doesn't?'

Rosina's expression became more disapproving. 'The way she put it to me once was that she had no intention of ruining her body for the sake of producing a little leech. Ingrid has a very clear sense of priorities, and number one on the list is herself.'

I sat in silence for a few seconds while I considered what I'd just been told. Could it be that Ingrid's interest in money had stimulated her to commit murder in the hope of seeing her husband take over Rodolfo's share of the business? Alternatively, had the 'very beautiful woman' fallen for the charms of her husband's cousin, only to be dumped when he met and married Alessia? Desertion can be a powerful motivator for murder. Something was for sure: I knew I wanted to sit down and talk to Ingrid sooner rather than later.

My conversation with Rosina continued and she told me more about her role in the business. From what she said, it was clear that *she* had been running the company, not her brother, and I felt sure she was a very capable woman. I also tended to believe what she said and I certainly came away from the meeting less likely to include her in a list of potential murder suspects.

But the same could not be said about Ingrid.

13

THURSDAY MORNING

The main police station in Verona is a modern concrete building on the banks of the river. I managed to find a parking space on the opposite pavement and as I walked over to the entrance with the precious plastic bag of evidence in my hands, I was amazed to see crowds of people queuing outside the security fence surrounding the station. From the languages I heard as I walked past them, it seemed likely that the majority if not all of these were asylum seekers. Luckily, I found a police constable by the main gate and I was able to explain that I had potentially important evidence relating to the death of Rodolfo Argento and he allowed me to jump the queue. He made a quick call and two minutes later, a female police officer emerged from the building and beckoned to me to accompany her. She led me inside and up two flights of stairs to a scene familiar to me after my years at Scotland Yard.

I found myself in a large open-plan office with desks either side of a central corridor and glazed offices every now and then to provide an element of privacy. She led me to one of these and I read the name *Ispettore Massimo Ventura* on the door.

'The inspector's in charge of the Argento enquiry. You can show him your evidence.'

Massimo Ventura looked up as I came in and waved towards a seat on the opposite side of a desk almost concealed beneath heaps of paperwork and I felt an immediate sense of camaraderie. It had been a standing joke in my office that nobody had ever seen the surface of my desk beneath its permanent covering of files. Ventura was probably ten years younger than me and he was completely bald. In an attempt to compensate, he had grown a beard, which covered his face and ended weirdly at ear level. I sat down and passed him across one of my cards. He took it from me and studied it for a few seconds before looking up.

'An English private investigator? That's unusual. I assume you're looking into the death of Rodolfo Argento. Is that correct?' I hastened to explain how a chance meeting with Violetta had got me involved with the case and he nodded. 'I had a feeling the old lady might want to go private. She was convinced that it was murder and she seemed to hold me personally responsible for not being able to prove it.'

I gave him a smile in return. 'Signora Violetta is a redoubtable character. She certainly knows her own mind. Anyway, what I've come to show you might be of interest.' I set the plastic bag on his desk and explained where I had found it while he listened intently before taking it from me.

'You're right, this could be very interesting. Can I take it that we aren't going to find your fingerprints on it?'

'Apart from possibly a print or two at the top when I first touched it in the bin, but I immediately used a tissue from then on and I can give you my prints for exclusion.'

He nodded approvingly. 'Very professional, Mr Armstrong. Tell me, what's your background? How come a Brit is working as a private investigator here in Italy?'

I filled him in with details of how I'd been a detective chief inspector in the murder squad at Scotland Yard until I'd decided to take early retirement and had moved to Tuscany. He looked up when I mentioned my former rank, 'Chief inspector, that's the equivalent of *commissario*, isn't it? That means you outrank me.'

I smiled back at him. 'That means I *used to* outrank you, Inspector. I've left the force now.'

'I'd be interested to hear your take on this case. I must confess that I've been suspicious from the start but I've been unable to get any proof of deliberate tampering. Forensics have been through the car – or what's left of it – with a magnifying glass but they can't find a thing. I just received a phone call this morning from the garage where the remains of the car have been taken and the guy there tells me he can't confirm or deny any interference with the brakes either.' He spread his hands helplessly.

'That would be Maurizio Tamburo. I visited him yesterday and saw the remains of the car for myself. In an ideal world, you might be lucky enough to find fingerprints on this oil can but, if not, I can quite understand that you'll just be scraping around for clues.'

'Do I take it that you share my opinion that it can't have been suicide?'

'Very definitely. Everybody I talk to tells me Rodolfo was in high spirits and looking forward to a major concert he would be performing in at Christmas. As far as I can tell, he was very happily married, at the top of his game professionally, and with no money problems. Can I ask you one thing: in the pathologist's report, was there any mention of an excess of alcohol or drugs in his system or some recurring medical problem that might have given him a temporary seizure? Or maybe some recent bad news, maybe a terminal diagnosis? Was he even on the phone at the time?'

He shook his head. 'His phone wasn't being used, there was

some alcohol in his system, but not enough to affect his driving, and nothing else. Certainly no history of epilepsy or anything like that and his doctor claimed he was very fit. So if we assume he didn't take his own life and it wasn't a simple accident, the question is who killed him and why? Who had motive and opportunity to do so?'

'And means. Although Maurizio at the garage told me it's a simple enough task to drain brake fluid, it's only simple if you're familiar with car engines, preferably classic cars.'

He nodded slowly. 'So we're looking for somebody with a working knowledge of cars, a strong motive for murder and who had the opportunity of getting into the garage to carry out the sabotage. That rather limits us to the people at the villa or the members of the Argento family.' He looked up. 'It probably won't come as any surprise to you to hear that when I mentioned this possibility to my *commissario*, he was very, very cautious. This is a very well-known and important family we're talking about, and if the news gets out that we suspect one of them of having committed murder, I can only begin to imagine the hornets' nest we would stir up.'

I gave him a sympathetic nod. 'I quite understand and I share your concern. This morning, I've been speaking to the victim's cousins, who currently run the Argento family business. I have to say that neither of them struck me as being potential murderers but anything's possible. They didn't in fact benefit from Rodolfo's death but I think it's reasonable to assume that they hoped they would. Whether this is sufficient for them to have considered murder is, of course, a totally different matter. So, as far as I can see, that leaves us with only a few other suspects.'

He was taking notes and ticking the names off on his file as I went through them. 'Go on, please.'

'There's Rodolfo's agent, Paolo Ruggieri, who was left a million euros in his will. I have yet to speak to him – although he's allegedly incapable of taking the top off a pen, let alone tampering with brakes in a classic car. There's the groundsman at the villa, who had a key to the garage and the opportunity and ability to drain the brake fluid but who, as far as I can tell, had absolutely no logical motive for wanting to kill his boss. Similarly, there's the manager of the villa, who has copies of all the keys but, again, I fail to see any possible motive there. There's a student at the academy who might or might not have crossed swords with the victim over some unidentified woman. I'll sit down and talk to the manager later today about him.'

He glanced up. 'Dolores Mendoza, I liked her. She seems very clued up and probably knows everything that goes on at the academy. Of course, she's a good-looking woman and apparently unattached, so I'm still leaving her on my list of possibles.'

I gave that some thought. He was right. Dolores was indeed an attractive woman and although she'd told me that she had rebuffed Rodolfo's advances, we had no proof of that. I liked her and automatically trusted her, but just because you like somebody doesn't mean they should be excluded from suspicion. I made a mental note to keep a close eye on her and her colleague, Clarissa. I nodded in agreement and continued.

'Yes, indeed, she certainly had access to the garage key, but nobody's made mention of her and the victim having been close. Of course, that doesn't mean it didn't happen. Then there's the principal, who gave me the impression that she maybe had a soft spot for the victim, and the same might be said of the woman behind the bar at Rodolfo's favourite café down by the lake. There's also Ingrid, the wife of Alfredo Argento. I haven't met her yet but she sounds like a very beautiful and potentially scheming sort of person who might or might not have been involved with the victim. Finally, there's the victim's wife, but after speaking to her last night, I got the impression the last thing she had on her mind would have been to kill him off – although she does know her way around classic car engines. She might be a very talented actor, but I tended to believe what she said.' I spread out my arms helplessly. 'Take your pick.'

After scribbling down or ticking off the names of the people I had identified, he pointed at the oil can in the bag in front of him. 'Like you say, in an ideal world, we find the fingerprints of the perpetrator on here, but, if not, it isn't going to be easy.' He glanced at his watch. 'I'll get this down to Forensics now and we should know pretty quickly whether there are any prints on it. If so, I'll come up to the villa this afternoon to take prints from everybody up there and I'll send somebody down to the couple who run the café by the lake. Before that, I think I'll go in person to the Agri Argento offices to get prints of Rosina and Alfredo Argento, as well as his wife if possible.'

He reached into a drawer and pulled out a familiar white card and a pad of ink. 'Just press your fingers on there for exclusion purposes, will you? For now, I'll just tell everybody the same thing: this is for exclusion only. I won't mention the oil can but taking prints is going to put the cat among the pigeons. I imagine most of the people have already made up their minds that it must have been an unfortunate accident. Discovering that we're treating it as murder will come as quite a shock to the system.' He looked up and gave me a wry grin. 'Starting with my boss. He isn't going to like that one bit. What about the scary old lady? I understood that she'd gone back to Tuscany. Any idea if she's going to be around?'

'Violetta told me she would be coming up for a board meeting scheduled for tomorrow. I seem to recall that she said she'll arrive this afternoon, but I suppose it might be tomorrow morning.' I gave him a grin as I wiped the ink off my fingers. 'Good luck taking her fingerprints. Give me a shout if you need backup.'

We both stood up and shook hands again. He gave me a friendly smile, thanked me for my help, and I promised he would be the first to know if I turned up anything else. We exchanged contact details so I had a direct line to him if necessary. He accompanied me downstairs to the main entrance and left me there. I returned to my van, relieved that the inspector had been prepared to accept input from a private eye – not always a given – and I set about looking for a better parking space. It took me about twenty minutes but finally I managed to squeeze the big vehicle into a gap in a narrow street in the old part of town where it looked as though I would have free parking for an hour. I called Anna and we arranged to meet up on the Ponte di Castelvecchio.

This fortified medieval bridge – also known as the Scaliger Bridge after the name of the ruling family responsible for building it – has crenelated battlements and is one of Verona's most famous landmarks. Built predominantly of ancient red bricks, it crosses the River Adige opposite the castle and is a Mecca for tourists. Sure enough, when I got there, the pedestrian bridge was heaving with people but I soon spotted Anna and Oscar just as he saw me and almost jerked her arm out of its socket in order to come charging over to greet me. While she massaged her shoulder, I took his lead from her. There was no point apologising. She and Oscar know each other well by now. She gave me a kiss on the cheek and enquired about the investigation. I told her it looked as though I had made a friend in the local police, which was a relief, but when I told her about my interviews with Alfredo and his sister, she shook her head sadly.

'So if they didn't do it, then who did? Surely not Alessia.'

'That's the million-dollar question. Maybe if we're really lucky, we'll get some prints off the oil can, but otherwise we're pretty much stuck.'

She must have heard the frustration in my voice because she

grabbed my arm with both of her hands and made a very sensible suggestion. 'I don't know about you, but I could really murder an ice cream. I spotted a very appealing-looking gelateria not far from here. Sound like a good idea to you?'

It did.

Ten minutes later, we were sitting at a table in a little piazza, shaded from the noonday sun by the buildings around us. Anna was obviously feeling hungrier than I was because she ordered what the menu described as a 'Tower of Chocolate' and I was most impressed to see her served something the size and shape of a bottle of beer, made up of milk, dark and white chocolate and smothered in whipped cream. In comparison, my black cherry, meringue and white chocolate mix looked almost pedestrian. I didn't forget Oscar either – he wouldn't have let me – and the waitress very kindly brought him some water and a couple of wafer biscuits. As we ate, Anna told me about her morning, walking around this beautiful city with Oscar. Obviously, because she had been with him, she hadn't been able to go into any of the churches, but I told her I would look after him this afternoon while I dropped her back into town to investigate the interior of the city's historic buildings to her heart's content.

I avoided talking about the case because it was just too frustrating for words at the moment. Although I was still hoping, I had a feeling that any killer worth his – or her – salt would have worn gloves so it wouldn't be easy to get any prints off the oil can and, without those, I wasn't really sure where we would go next. There remained the very unpalatable possibility that no perpetrator would ever be found, and the murder of Rodolfo Argento would remain forever unsolved – if indeed it had been murder, and we couldn't even prove that yet.

14

THURSDAY AFTERNOON

The clothes of our fellow diners at lunch were less colourful than the previous day but the food still of a very high standard: seafood risotto followed by roast chicken and roast potatoes. There were no more costumes and no bursts of song and we found ourselves sharing the table with Dolores, while Elektra sprawled at our feet with Oscar resting his head on her back. He was clearly delighted to meet his new friend again, while I was glad to have the opportunity of speaking to Dolores. I started by giving her my news. If she was the killer, this would do no harm, and if she was innocent, I felt sure I could trust her to keep her mouth shut for the moment until the results of the fingerprints came back.

'It could be that I've found proof that Rodolfo was murdered. It seems increasingly likely that somebody tampered with the brakes of his car. I've spoken to the police inspector in charge of the case and he agrees with me. This of course brings us back to the question of who might have done it. Do you have any thoughts?'

She stared at me in disbelief. 'Rodolfo, really murdered? Are you sure?' As a reaction, it struck me as genuine.

'I'm afraid that's the way it looks.' At that moment, my phone bleeped and I saw that it was a text message from Inspector Ventura. It was brief and to the point.

One clear set of prints on the oil can apart from yours and the victim's. Going to Agri Argento offices and then coming to the villa to take prints from everyone this afternoon. Please inform them.

I looked up at Dolores. 'Are you sure you can't think of anybody with a grudge against Rodolfo, anybody who previously threatened him? Maybe a woman or a jealous man?' I was clutching at straws but I knew I had to try.

'I honestly can't.' She looked around the room and lowered her voice. 'Before he got married, it's true that he did have a few romantic involvements with women here. At the time, I know there was quite a lot of bad blood between him and one or two of the people here but ever since his marriage, I'm pretty sure all that had stopped. If it was somebody with a grudge, I can't see why they would have waited so long to take action.'

'Can you give me any names? I promise I won't mention you when I interview the people.'

'I'd really rather not but if you insist, the most obvious is Romeo – he's been coming every summer for three years now. He had a thing for a girl called Rosanna two years ago but it was quite clear to most of us that Rodolfo was carrying on with her. We could all see that Romeo was very unhappy with the way things worked out but, like I say, that was ages ago.'

I sat back and considered what I'd just been told. Could it be that Romeo had waited until now to exact his revenge – and if so, why? There remained the question of whether he would have had the expertise to drain the brake fluid from the Jaguar, but I made a mental note to look into that.

'I believe that on the day of the accident, Romeo and Rodolfo had an argument after Romeo made a sexist comment about Alessia's blouse. Does that ring a bell?'

'Not that particular incident, but it doesn't surprise me. Romeo loves being outrageous. I heard him tell Clarissa the other day that her bottom looked like a Roman statue. He really doesn't care what he says.'

'And how did Clarissa respond to that?'

'She did her best to laugh it off and told him to keep his comments to himself. She knows him well by now. This is his third summer here but, to be honest, he seems to be getting more outrageous every year, so this might be the last time he gets a place on the course.'

I glanced around and, seeing as we weren't being overheard, I asked a more delicate question.

'I promise I won't quote you on this and I apologise if the question makes you feel awkward, but when I interviewed Clarissa this morning, I very much got the impression that she liked Rodolfo... a lot.'

Dolores blushed red and, just as I had done, took a careful look around before answering. 'I don't know who initiated it or how far it went, but I'm sure there was something going on between them the winter before last. They were very circumspect, but I could tell.'

'Thank you and I promise I won't mention your name in connection with this. The winter before last, you say? Have you any idea what brought the relationship to an end?'

'That's easy – the appearance of Alessia on the scene. Rodolfo first met Alessia around Easter of last year and from the moment he first saw her, it was clear to everybody that he was completely hooked.'

'How did Clarissa take that? I presume she wasn't very happy about it.'

Dolores took another quick look around. 'Like I say, they had been very careful to hide the relationship, but obviously it broke her heart. She was in a terrible state for months.'

'Do you think she might have borne a grudge until now?'

'And then decided to kill him?' Dolores looked at me wide-eyed. 'Absolutely not. Clarissa hasn't got a violent bone in her body. No, I think she just nursed her broken heart and gradually got over it, though she never stopped loving him. Certainly since hearing the news of his death, she's been distraught. She does her best to hide it, but I can tell she's bleeding inside. I'm sure it came as a terrible blow to her, just as it did to the rest of us.'

I filed this information away for further consideration, making a mental note that Dolores's comments had pointed a finger of suspicion at the principal. Was she telling the truth or was this maybe an attempt at disinformation to deviate attention from herself? I left it at that for now and informed Dolores that everybody was going to have their fingerprints taken this afternoon. She looked shocked and immediately stood up.

'I think I'd better make an announcement now so that everybody's prepared. Some people might be quite frightened when they see the police descending on the villa. I suppose I'd better break the news at the same time that the police are treating Rodolfo's death as suspicious. That will come as a major shock, I'm sure. Is it all right for me to do that?'

I told her to go ahead and a few seconds later, she was tapping a spoon against a glass to get the attention of everybody. While she explained what would be happening, I did my best to study the faces around me, particularly that of Romeo. I read shock, apprehension and disbelief on many faces but I couldn't see any immediate signs of guilt on his or any of the others'. While I still intended to keep Romeo on my list of suspects, the lack of guilty faces made it more likely that Rodolfo Argento's killer was one of our far smaller pool of suspects.

When Dolores returned to the table, I changed the subject to keys. 'I know I've asked you this before, but can you think of any way anybody else could have got hold of the key to the garage? You've already told me that your master key was firmly locked in the safe. Are you sure you didn't leave that open at any time?'

She shook her head. 'Absolutely not. I always keep it locked and the combination is only known to me and Clarissa.'

'What about the other keys? Might Beppe have left his key in his jacket unattended, do you think?'

'I doubt it; I know he's very careful about that sort of thing. I suppose, to be honest, the most likely person to have left the key hanging around was Rodolfo himself. When he worked in the garage, I often saw him take off his jacket and hang it up while he pulled on his overalls. I suppose somebody could have got hold of the key then.'

This thought had already occurred to me but there was a potential problem. 'But a remote control isn't like an ordinary key. It isn't so easy to make a copy... or is it?'

Dolores knew the answer. 'In fact, it is. There are numerous places in Verona where they can do it on the spot in a matter of minutes. I got a copy done last year when Beppe ran over his with the tractor.' This was news to me and it simplified things for a would-be killer.

'Might Rodolfo have left the garage unattended at any time?'

'You'd better ask Beppe, but the answer is probably yes. When he was fiddling with the cars, Rodolfo often took them for short test drives and I'm pretty sure he didn't always bother to lock the garage door while he was out. I suppose somebody might have been able to sneak in while he was away and tamper with the Jaguar's brakes.'

I listened with interest. By the sound of it, almost anybody here could have seized the opportunity to take the remote control, copy it, and return it to Rodolfo's pocket without him being any the wiser. I did a quick calculation. Depending where the killer took the remote to be copied, he or she would have needed half an hour to get there and back plus however long the job took. So, realistically, the murderer would only have needed forty minutes or so. If Rodolfo had been working on one of his cars, it was very likely that his jacket would have been hanging up for at least an hour, if not more, so it was very feasible. What this meant was that the would-be killer could have stolen Rodolfo's key and copied it days, weeks before. Needless to say, this didn't help in narrowing down the list of suspects.

Dolores looked across at me helplessly. 'But who could have done it?'

Who indeed?

* * *

That afternoon, I dropped Anna back down to the centre of Verona and while I was there, I decided to check out Paolo Ruggieri, Rodolfo's theatrical agent. With the help of Google, I located his office in a smart apartment block in the more modern part of town where, thankfully, parking was a lot easier than in the old town. I had Oscar with me and we had a little walk around first, enjoying the shade of some lovely old trees lining the sides of the wide boulevard. When we got to the apartment block, I checked the names alongside the bells by the front door. Sure enough, one of these was marked Ruggieri, prefixed by the words *Agente Teatrale* so I pressed it and waited. A quick check of my watch told me that it was barely half past two so maybe he was having a long lunch or a siesta. I was just about to try a second time when a metallic voice croaked at me out of the speaker.

'Yes, who is it?' It was a woman's voice and she sounded half asleep. Maybe I had interrupted her lunch break.

'Hello, my name is Armstrong. I'm investigating the murder of Rodolfo Argento and I'd like to speak to Mr Ruggieri, Paolo Ruggieri, please.'

'I'm sorry, did you say "murder"? I thought Rodolfo's death was an accident.' She certainly sounded wide awake now.

'Apparently not. Is Mr Ruggieri there?'

'No, but I'm expecting him back any time now. Would you like to come up and wait? We're on the fourth floor.'

There was a buzzing noise and the front door sprang open. I took the lift up to the fourth floor and when Oscar and I stepped out of it, we found ourselves directly opposite a door emblazoned with the name of the agent in gold letters. I knocked and we went inside.

We were greeted by a woman, probably only a few years younger than me, but who had obviously been striving a lot harder than I had to put off the ageing process for as long as possible. Her dazzling blonde hair looked too good to be true – and probably was. Her face was plastered with a thick coating of make-up and her bright-red lipstick highlighted recently overfilled lips. It wouldn't have been a look I would have chosen, but I couldn't blame her for wanting to hold back the ravages of time. I gave her a friendly smile and her eyes lit up when she spotted Oscar.

'Oh, what a beautiful dog. What's her name?'

For a moment, he exchanged glances with me and I hastened to introduce him properly. 'Good afternoon. This is Oscar, he's only three and he's a bit excitable so he'll probably try to climb on your lap if you let him.'

She didn't seem to mind and he wandered over willingly so she could make a fuss of him. Fortunately, he didn't try and climb on her lap, which was probably just as well because, from what I could see of the skirt she was wearing, it was little wider than a belt and I feared she could have got scratched if he had tried. She waved me into a seat on one of a pair of armchairs at the side of the room and reached for the phone.

'Can I get you a coffee?'

I thanked her and asked for an espresso. She phoned the local bar and placed the order before returning her attention to me. 'Are you with the police?'

'I'm working alongside the local police but I'm actually a private investigator engaged by Signora Violetta Argento to discover the truth of what happened.'

'So what makes you think it was murder?'

I had only just started my explanation when there was a noise at the door and a man appeared. Although I had never met a theatrical agent in my life, one look at this character told me that I had to be in the presence of Paolo Ruggieri. In spite of the hot weather outside, he was wearing a long, dark-blue, velvet jacket, not dissimilar to the kind of thing Teddy boys used to wear back in the fifties. Instead of a tie, he was sporting a cravat in a bold paisley pattern principally consisting of pinks and greys. There was a matching handkerchief in his top pocket that spilled out halfway down his front. He was certainly memorable and even Oscar stared at him in amazement.

The blonde bombshell was quick to introduce me.

'Paolo, this gentleman is Mr Armstrong. He's a private investigator and he says that Rodolfo Argento was murdered. It wasn't an accident at all.'

The air of bonhomie on the face of the theatrical agent disappeared in a flash, to be replaced by a pasty look. As he tottered over and slumped into the other armchair opposite me, I heard his secretary make another call to the café. 'And a double espresso with a large shot of brandy in it.'

Ruggieri sat there for a few moments, studying his hands, before looking up at me, his expression almost beseeching. 'That can't be right, surely. Who on earth would have wanted to murder Rodolfo?'

'That's what I've been engaged to discover, Mr Ruggieri. Can you think of anybody who might have wished him harm? Did he have any enemies? I've already been told that a year or two ago, he had a reputation as a womaniser, but I've also been told that since his marriage, he appeared to have calmed right down again. Does that sound right to you?'

The answer came from the blonde and I was immediately interested that she appeared to know the opera singer so intimately. 'He used to be a terror, ask anybody. But whoever told you he calmed down when he married Alessia was dead right. He was a changed man after he met her.'

'So if his murder wasn't as a result of his philandering, who could it have been?'

The theatrical agent shook his head slowly. 'I have no idea. I'm sorry, but I just can't believe it. He was a national treasure. Why would anybody wish him dead?'

'You can't think of any enemies, jealous rivals, other singers he might have eclipsed and who bore a grudge?'

He just kept shaking his head.

'I've been told that a day or two before his death, you and he had a furious argument on the phone. Can you tell me what that was all about, please?'

He and his receptionist exchanged glances and I felt sure I could see her give him a little nod, as much as to say, *You might as well.*

His shoulders slumped and he kept his attention on his hands as he spoke. 'We were arguing about money.' I made no comment and waited for him to continue. 'For the last ten years, he's been paying me twelve and a half per cent commission on bookings that I get for him. You know what it's like trying to make ends meet these days. Everything's been shooting up in price so I decided I had to ask him if he could increase it to at least 15 per cent. Most other agents routinely charge 20 per cent.' He gave me a beseeching look. 'Surely fifteen's not too much to ask?'

'And he said no?'

To my surprise, he shook his head. 'No, he told me he needed to speak to his mother first. He always consulted her about everything. I'm afraid I knew from experience how that would have ended. There would have been as much chance of getting a pay rise out of her as of me appearing on stage singing a duet alongside Rodolfo. I couldn't help myself and I just lost it. I told him in no uncertain terms that I was fed up with her interference. I'm afraid I said some pretty harsh things about her being too old, too mean and past it. I should have known better, I did know better, but, stupidly, I didn't stop and think. Rodolfo went ballistic.' Ruggieri looked across at me and offered a few words of explanation that didn't come as a surprise to me. 'He and his mother had an unbelievably close relationship – some might say it was far too close – and he wouldn't hear a bad word about her.'

'How did the conversation end?'

'He slammed the phone down on me and that was the last I heard of it. Two days later, he was dead. You can imagine how awful I felt later when I heard that he'd left me a million euros in his will. A million euros! I should have known that he was a generous man and I shouldn't have doubted him.'

'The money came as a surprise to you? He had never mentioned this before?'

'Never. I didn't think for one moment I would get a mention of any kind in his will.'

He sounded convincing enough, but I couldn't help thinking to myself that this telephone argument might have been a whole lot more acrimonious than he was saying. What if Rodolfo had told his agent about the bequest and then, as a result of the man's outburst, had threatened to change the terms of his will to cut him out? Knowing he was about to lose a million euros might have stimulated the flamboyant Paolo Ruggieri to take radical action.

A few seconds later, there was a tap at the door and our coffees arrived. I was still reaching for mine when Ruggieri grabbed hold of his cup and upended it into his mouth. He looked dejected and bewildered, but the fact remained that he had just catapulted himself up my list of suspects. Whether this would result in my being able to prove his involvement in the singer's death was another matter completely, but the agent had certainly managed to get himself top billing on my list.

15

THURSDAY AFTERNOON

I spent the afternoon wandering around Verona with Oscar. Leaving the car where it was, we walked back to the river and followed it for a mile or so as it curled around the old town before we crossed over a bridge and headed into the narrow streets. One thing I soon discovered was that for anybody riding a bike in Verona – and there were lots of them – the older the bike, the better. Because the streets are mainly paved with square cobbles or flagstones, the battered old bikes bump around on the uneven surfaces, creak, squeak and generally provide advanced warning of their arrival. I kept Oscar on the lead all the same but he seemed quite happy to walk at my side and take in the view just as I did. We ended up in the beautiful Piazza delle Erbe with its statues, ancient frescoes and fountains, and I had no hesitation in heading for a gelateria where we sat down at a table shaded by an umbrella.

I sent a message to Anna giving her our location and to my surprise, only about five minutes later, just as my strawberry, apricot and peach ice cream arrived, so did Anna. She was quick to order an ice-cream selection for herself and then she told me all about her afternoon of historical investigation. She had started at the Castelvecchio museum and then had taken in the cathedral with its painting of the Assumption, allegedly by Titian, followed by the Basilica of San Zeno, which has been in existence for over a thousand years. This church is also the legendary site of the marriage of Romeo and Juliet, but for Anna who only believes in facts, this was of little interest. I've often thought that in many ways she would make an excellent detective – facts are the only things that count for us, too.

When she brought the conversation around to my investigation, I gave her a quick rundown of my visit to Rodolfo's agent and added my impression that he might have been the perpetrator. Interestingly, she was fascinated to hear of the showy blonde receptionist and queried whether I thought there might have been something going on between her and the opera singer in spite of the age difference between them. I shrugged my shoulders, but it occurred to me that there had been a wedding ring on her finger, and I wondered whether maybe she was actually married to the agent. If so, and if she had been carrying on with Rodolfo, this served to push the agent even further up my list of suspects. But without clear proof, all I could do for now was shrug my shoulders once more and hold my hands up helplessly.

'Maybe she and Rodolfo were an item once upon a time, but everybody seems to agree that from when Rodolfo met Alessia last year, he was a changed man.'

'And you believe that?'

I nodded but she didn't look convinced – and neither was I. She reinforced her point.

'In my experience, the leopard doesn't always change his spots as easily as that.'

I nodded again. I couldn't have said it better myself.

* * *

It was half past five by the time we got back to the villa, and the first things I saw were a pair of blue and white police squad cars parked outside the front door. I was just letting Oscar out of the van when Beppe the groundsman appeared on the steps, wiping his fingers on a cloth. He looked up and walked over to me with a smile.

'Well, that's a first. I've never had my fingerprints taken before. In fairness, the police are being very respectful and none of the residents seem to be too worried.'

'Did you see the police inspector in there: black beard and a shaved head?'

'Yes, he's in the hall talking to Dolores. Any progress?'

'It's looking more and more like murder, but we still aren't sure. That's what the fingerprints are for.'

'Well, good luck and remember, if I can help in any way, just ask.'

I thanked him and went inside. Sure enough, Massimo Ventura was standing there accompanied by Dolores, Elektra the Labrador and a young constable. While Oscar hurried over to renew his friendship with the other Lab, we humans shook hands and I introduced Anna. Dolores tactfully withdrew – but, interestingly, Elektra stayed here with Oscar – and I was able to talk to Ventura without fear of being overheard. The inspector told us that they had almost finished taking prints here, and that one of his men was at the home of Alfredo Argento at this very moment taking prints from his decidedly recalcitrant wife. He gave me a little wink. 'It would be so good if we could get a match.'

I told him what Dolores had told me about Romeo, as well as what she had said about Rodolfo getting together with Clarissa, only for the relationship to come to an end when he met Alessia. I also gave him the gist of my conversation with the theatrical agent and his receptionist and he immediately gave orders for a car to be sent to take their prints as well. After thanking me, he changed the subject. 'By the way, Dolores told me that you have a key to the garage. I wonder if you could show me exactly where you found the oil can and so on.'

Anna opted to go up to the room so the inspector and I went out, accompanied by the two dogs and the constable. We walked around the side of the villa and I opened the garage door. Both men gave appreciative grunts when they saw the amazing line-up of classic cars. Inspector Ventura stared around in awe.

'This is what I call a hobby! He was a lucky man: so much money, an amazing collection like this, a beautiful, talented wife, and this unbelievable villa. If I'd still been harbouring any thoughts of him having taken his own life, I'm certainly not now.'

I showed them where the Jaguar had usually been parked and pointed out how it looked very much to me as if somebody had run a mop over the concrete fairly recently. After that, I took them to the workbench and pointed out the rubbish bag where I had found the oil can. The inspector gave instructions to the constable, who pulled on a pair of disposable gloves and began to empty the bag piece by piece onto the worktop. All the other containers in there were empty but he did find one piece of interesting evidence. This was a dirty rag, still slightly damp, clearly having been soaked with something viscous. When I leant down to smell it, I was in little doubt.

'For my money, this is brake fluid. Might this be the cloth that was used to clean up underneath the Jaguar?'

The inspector nodded. 'Could well be. Wouldn't it be nice if we could find some DNA on here? If so, then we're going to have to come back and swab everybody for DNA but let's see if there's anything to be found first.'

While the constable bagged the evidence, the inspector and I wandered around accompanied by the two sniffing dogs, checking door and window locks, but without finding anything untoward. It looked very likely that if somebody had tampered with the brakes they must have got in either with the key or during a brief interval while the door had been left open while Rodolfo had gone out. But who?

We were just leaving the garage when another police officer arrived, looking uneasy. He spoke quietly to the inspector, who glanced across at me and raised his eyebrows. 'Now, why doesn't this come as a surprise? Signora Violetta Argento has just arrived and she's objecting violently to being asked to provide fingerprints. I wonder if you'd mind accompanying me, Mr Armstrong. You know her better than I do. I think I'm going to need backup.'

I waited until the garage door was once again securely locked before following the inspector around to the villa entrance. We found Violetta in the hall with a face like thunder. Fortunately, the arrival of the two dogs appeared to cheer her, at least briefly, and I decided to help the inspector by getting a few words in first.

'Good evening, Signora Violetta, I hope you've had a good journey. As you've probably realised, it's looking increasingly likely that your son was indeed murdered as you thought and, in consequence, the police are taking fingerprints from everybody here at the villa for exclusion purposes.'

She shot me a suspicious look. 'And just what exactly does "exclusion purposes" mean?'

I was impressed to hear the inspector bravely join in. 'Exactly what it says, Signora Argento. We believe we might have found some meaningful prints that could lead us to the identity of the murderer, and so it's vitally important that we take prints from everybody here so they can be excluded from the investigation. This doesn't necessarily mean that we consider anybody here to be a suspect. Certainly, there's no question of me considering *you* as a suspect.'

She appeared at least partially mollified by this and, although still under protest, she allowed the sergeant to take her prints. As this took place, I gave her a quick summary of my enquiries so far, just saying that the brakes appeared to have been tampered with but without specifically mentioning the container of brake fluid. From the expression on her face, I could see that she was struggling. On the one hand, she was evidently pleased that her hunch looked as though it had been proved right but now, as it sank in, she found herself having to confront the fact that her precious son really had been murdered. I did my best to keep her talking and suggested that we go for a cold beer. This suggestion was met with approval not only from her but also from the inspector, and we walked through to the bar area. There were very few people here at this time of day and we sat down at a table to one side where we could talk freely. Oscar stretched out on the floor alongside Elektra with his head once more on her shoulder in a picture of domestic bliss. Violetta gradually relaxed as well and by the time the beers arrived, she was actually able to propose a little toast.

'Thank you, gentlemen, for your efforts. When are you planning on making the arrest?'

I let the inspector answer this one. 'Our main problem has been one of motive. Although it's clear that your son almost certainly made himself unpopular in the past because of his treatment of women, people seem to agree that, since getting married, all that had finally stopped. So, if this wasn't a crime of passion, what other motive might be behind it?'

Violetta took a sip of beer before addressing me, rather than the inspector. 'I already told you, Mr Armstrong. I have no doubt at all who the murderer was. Didn't you tell the inspector? Why haven't you arrested her yet?'

I did my best to reply tactfully. 'The inspector needs evidence before he can arrest anybody.'

But Violetta wasn't giving up without a fight. 'Alessia was here that day and she could easily have tampered with his car. She knows about old cars. She knew that by killing Rodolfo, she would become very rich and she could be with all the men she wanted. Surely that's all the motive you need.'

The inspector, to his credit, demonstrated that he wasn't afraid to raise his head above the parapet. 'But she wasn't the only one to gain from your son's death, was she? The same argument about money could be applied to his cousins – even if they were ultimately to be disappointed – his agent, and even you, Signora.'

A stony silence fell on the table for almost a minute before Violetta looked up at him in disbelief.

'One of us? Are you seriously suggesting that one of the family might have killed Rodolfo? It's unthinkable and it's insulting. We are a respectable family, and respectable families don't go around committing murder.'

Tell that to Hamlet, I wisely decided not to say out loud.

16

THURSDAY EVENING

I was glad to get back to our suite. From the look of him, Oscar was also delighted – even if it meant separation from his new girlfriend – as he headed straight for his basket and settled into it with a thud. Anna and I both lay down on the bed and I closed my eyes gratefully, Violetta's words still echoing in my head: *Respectable families don't go around committing murder.*

As a general rule, of course, she was quite right, but that didn't alter the fact that time after time in my career in the police I had come across apparently respectable people who had nevertheless been able to commit atrocious crimes. As far as families were concerned, these crimes had all too often been provoked by money. I lay back and thought about the current situation in the Argento family. Violetta had no shortage of money – a share in the business, the villa in Tuscany and the villa here in Verona plus whatever else she had inherited from her son and, of course, her original, no doubt substantial fortune. What would happen if something happened to her?

Although I knew it was going to be difficult, this was a question I was going to have to ask her sooner rather than later. Could it possibly be that somebody had deliberately murdered her son, knowing that half of his fortune would revert to her, with a view to then killing her as well so as to get their hands on everything? Of course, that all depended on the terms of her will. Who would benefit from her death? It was clear from what she had said that she wasn't a fan of Alfredo, but Agri Argento was a family business, after all, and I knew that tradition meant a lot to her. I couldn't see her leaving it to anybody not connected with the company, and that no doubt included Alessia, so that almost certainly meant the cousins would inherit. Could they really have been behind Rodolfo's death?

But, more significantly now, did this mean that Violetta was going to be our next murder victim?

I was roused from my deliberations by the sound of a doorbell. I hadn't even realised that our suite had a bell and this one reproduced the chimes of Big Ben. I opened the door to find myself faced by none other than Signora Violetta.

'I hope I'm not disturbing you, Mr Armstrong. I wondered if you and your girlfriend might like to come for an *aperitivo* a bit later on? Say seven o'clock? You know where my apartment is, don't you?'

And that was that.

I went back to the bedroom and told Anna that we had been summoned. A glance at my watch told me it was already six-thirty so we hurriedly showered and changed. While getting ready, I rehearsed the best way of breaking the news to Violetta that her life might be in danger – most probably from a member of her own family – and I had a feeling it wasn't going to go down too well.

At seven o'clock on the dot, we walked back along the corridor to Violetta's apartment and rang the doorbell. She waved us in and led us into a delightful, airy living room with French windows that opened onto the roof terrace. It came as no surprise at all to see three bottles of Beck's sitting on a tray by the door. Although the view from the terrace was stunning, directly down over Lake Garda, it was completely exposed to the sun and that still had a lot of warmth in it. Realising this, Violetta pointed at Oscar and shook her head.

'It's probably best if we stay inside. I'm sure your dog doesn't like too much direct sunlight.'

I nodded in agreement. 'Nor me. After all, I am English.'

We took our drinks and sat down in front of a magnificent, sculpted marble fireplace with a portrait of a man hanging above it. No prizes for guessing who this was. I had by now seen enough photos of her son to recognise the handsome chap in the dinner jacket. The mantelpiece was covered in photos of mother and son together, from him as a baby to him as a star on stage, mementoes ranging from gold medals to framed certificates – naturally for singing – and a series of cards and candles. There was even a – to my eyes – rather tacky heart-shaped silver frame with a photo of the great man in it and the words *I love you* written across it. I felt a pang of sympathy for the grieving mother. I read the wording on some of the cards and soon saw that they were mostly good luck cards from mother to son or congratulations on some operatic achievement. Presumably, he had saved them and now she was exhibiting them for her own sake. It was very touching – if slightly macabre.

Anna duly admired the painting. 'What a lovely portrait of your son. How long ago was that painted?'

An expression of acute grief crossed Violetta's face. 'Barely three months ago. I had two of them done from a photo of him on stage at La Scala in Milan. The other one is hanging in the Montevolpone villa.'

We sat in silence and sipped our drinks for a while before

Violetta returned to more practical matters. 'I'm very concerned that the inspector doesn't seem to be taking my accusations seriously. Surely any fool can see that Alessia has to be the murderer. Can't you see it, Mr Armstrong?'

What I could see quite clearly was that Violetta was trying to divide and rule. It was evident that she had little or no time for Inspector Ventura, while my impression of him had been of a good, professional police officer. I did my best to reply tactfully, but firmly.

'As we said earlier, the inspector can't arrest somebody without proof and the problem we have at the moment is that there's no proof against Alessia... or anybody else.' I swallowed a quick mouthful of beer for Dutch courage. 'And to be perfectly honest with you, I don't share your opinion of her. From everything I've heard from other people and from talking to her myself, she and your son had a loving relationship and everybody agrees that he appeared to be a changed man from the moment he met her. Just as importantly, nobody has so much as hinted at any infidelity on her part either.'

I looked up and caught her eye for a moment.

'Nobody, that is, apart from you, Signora Violetta. When I spoke to you last Sunday, you told me you were convinced Alessia had been having affairs, but the only justification you could give me was – if I remember correctly – that she was "far too good-looking for her own good". That, as I'm sure you're fully aware, is not the sort of allegation that would stand up in a court of law. Can you give me some kind of proof to substantiate what you said or are you prepared to accept that maybe you might be wrong about her?'

I buried my nose in my glass and waited for the explosion but, in fact, I had to wait almost a minute for a response from her.

When it came, it was unexpectedly mild and I listened in fascination.

'People say that there's a special relationship between a mother and her son and that's certainly what I had with Rodolfo. He was an amazing boy.' There was a wistful note in her voice that must have got through to my four-legged friend because Oscar got up and wandered across to sit alongside her with his nose on her lap. She looked down and stroked his ears distractedly as she picked up her story again. 'He started singing and playing the piano when he was four – and I don't just mean sitting at the keyboard and randomly striking the keys – and even from that early age, it was clear that he had the voice of an angel. Only a year later, my husband died and my whole world became centred on Rodolfo. I hardly let him out of my sight until he was well into his teens and I did everything I could to nurture his talent and give him every chance to become the greatest opera singer of all time.' She looked up with tears in her eyes 'And he would have been, you know. He just needed a few more years of experience and he would have been the greatest of the greats.'

Anna made a few encouraging noises but I stayed out of it for now and just waited for Violetta to pick up again. It didn't take long.

'We had a wonderful close relationship right up until he first developed an interest in the opposite sex.' There was frustration and anger in her voice now. 'Those girls almost ruined him completely, and from then on, I found myself constantly fighting to keep him away from unsuitable women who would only lead him astray.'

I caught Anna's eye for a moment and it was immediately clear that she was thinking along the same lines as I was: unpicking the relationship between Rodolfo Argento and his mum would have been a psychotherapist's dream – or nightmare. Hopefully unaware of the thoughts going through my head, Violetta continued.

'I guided him, I nurtured him, I ensured that he had the best tuition money could buy and I loved him; I loved him deeply and sincerely as only a mother can. Coming back to what you were just saying, if I'm being totally honest, I would have to admit that I didn't really mind all the affairs he was having because I knew that was just a physical urge he needed to satisfy. When Alessia came along, everything changed and I knew that I'd lost him.' The forlorn note in her voice had now been replaced by something more feral. 'She took him away from me. How do you expect me to feel about her?'

Her voice tailed off into silence. I gave it a few moments before adding my own comments. 'It was easier for you to think of her as an evil monster than to accept the fact that your son could love somebody else as intensely, or even more intensely, than he had his own mother. I can understand how that might have made you feel.'

As I said it, I couldn't help wondering whether maybe this change of heart in her son might have engendered a sense of such bitter disappointment in her that I might be looking at his murderer now. No sooner had the thought crossed my mind than I discounted it. After all, this was the woman who had deliberately brought me into the case because she had felt sure he had been murdered. Certainly, that would hardly have been logical behaviour for the real murderer. She relapsed into silence and I waited some time for her to speak again before deciding that now was as good a time as any to ask about her will.

'I'd like to ask you a very personal question, Signora Violetta, but I want you to know that the only reason I'm asking it is because this could potentially be very important in solving the mystery of who killed your son. I guarantee you that this information will go no further than myself or, with your permission, the police inspector. Please could you tell me if you have made a will?'

She looked up sharply. 'Of course I have. What kind of idiot do you take me for?'

'I was sure you would have done, but I'd be very grateful if you could tell me the terms of your will. What would happen if you passed away tomorrow?'

I had to wait almost a minute before she gave me her answer and I was just beginning to think that she was going to refuse my request when she started speaking. 'That question has been exercising me a lot over the past few years and, of course, since Rodolfo's death, even more so.' She looked up from her hands and gave me a hard stare. 'I trust you, Mr Armstrong. Don't betray my trust. This is highly confidential.'

Anna, taking the hint, stood up. 'I think I'll just go out on the terrace and have a look at the view for a few minutes. It's too beautiful an evening for staying inside. Oscar, feel like coming with me?'

I gave her a grateful smile and watched as she and Oscar went out into the evening sunshine. No sooner had they done so than Violetta started speaking again.

'I saw my lawyer and changed the terms of my will only a week ago. This villa here already belongs to the AOA Foundation but I intend to leave the foundation sufficient funds for them to keep operating and perpetuating Rodolfo's memory. I see absolutely no reason why I should give anything to Alfredo and Rosina so, as far as the rest is concerned, I have no alternative but to leave everything to Tosca.'

'Tosca?'

There was silence for a couple of seconds before she broke the news to me.

'My daughter.'

This was so unexpected that I probably sounded quite gormless. 'You have a daughter? I didn't know.' I very nearly snapped at her that it would have been nice to have known about this before but I controlled myself and waited for her to respond. What was going through my head was that a very strong new suspect had appeared out of the blue. Had one sibling killed the other, either out of jealousy or so as to get hands on the family fortune when their mother died?

There was another long pause before Violetta spoke. 'Tosca and I don't have a close relationship. In fact, apart from a glimpse of her at Rodolfo's wedding and then again at his funeral, I haven't seen her for seven years, not since my brother's funeral.'

'You aren't in touch with each other?'

She shook her head, but I couldn't work out whether this was with regret or just acknowledging the status quo. 'She left home when she was eighteen and I've probably seen her no more than four or five times in the intervening eighteen years and spoken to her two or three times at most. And that was fine by me.'

There was a stubborn edge to her voice and I realised, not for the first time, that Violetta had a tough, unforgiving streak.

17

THURSDAY EVENING

Anna and I went back to our room at just before seven-thirty so that I could feed Oscar, and while I did so, I revealed what Violetta had told me. Anna was as surprised as I had been to hear of Tosca, the daughter, and both of us were soon confronting the same problem. Violetta had told me nothing more about her daughter and I desperately wanted to find out as much as possible about her, mainly because, in the event of something happening to her mother, it now seemed clear that the mysterious Tosca was likely to inherit a massive fortune – the sort of incredible wealth that could easily provide a motive for murder. Could it be that the daughter had killed her brother, knowing that half his wealth would pass to his wife, but the other half would go to their mother and then to herself? If so, then the next step in Tosca's plan would surely be to eliminate Violetta too.

I had been so surprised by this latest turn of events that I had held back from suggesting to Violetta that she might be in danger, but I knew that I urgently needed to speak to her daughter. Before going down for dinner, I phoned Inspector Ventura and gave him this latest piece of news. With the facilities of the police, he should be able to locate the woman far more easily than I could. As an afterthought, I dictated the name of Violetta's Hungarian husband in case Tosca had decided to revert to that name after splitting from her mother. Ventura thanked me most warmly and promised to let me know if he managed to locate her. He agreed with me that she had now suddenly become a person of considerable interest in this case.

Anna and I arrived downstairs just as the gong was sounding for dinner and we joined the throng making their way into the dining room. As we did so, we bumped into Alessia, who invited us to sit with her. I was secretly delighted about this as it would hopefully give me the opportunity to quiz her about her husband's sister.

After a starter of mixed salami, accompanied by sundried tomatoes and olives, we moved on to gnocchi. The potato dumplings were smothered with butter and melted cheese and I had no trouble at all in wolfing down my plateful under the baleful gaze of my dog, who clearly felt unreasonably excluded. Half a packet of breadsticks went some way towards pacifying him, but I had to admit that he missed a real treat. I felt understandably full after this feast and I was greatly relieved to find that we were then served a relatively light main course of cold salmon and a mixed salad, which was perfect.

Understandably, Alessia was keen to know how the investigation was progressing, and I told her as much as I felt I should, emphasising the fact that, unless the fingerprint evidence came up with something conclusive, we still had no firm suspects. When I felt the moment was right, I gently approached the subject of Rodolfo's newly discovered sister.

'I was talking to Violetta earlier and she mentioned that she has a daughter. Can you tell me anything about Tosca?'

She looked up from her plate with an expression of pity on her face. 'Such a shame. I'm sure Tosca's very bright but her mother didn't give her a chance. All her life, she lived in the shadow of her big brother and what she needed the most – maternal love – never came her way. As far as I can work out, she was born around about the time her father died and I think his death probably tipped Violetta over the edge. From then on, Violetta only had eyes for her boy, the Wunderkind, and the new baby didn't get a look-in. I've only seen Tosca twice – at my wedding and then at Rodolfo's funeral, so you can imagine how brief our conversations were.'

'Do you happen to know where she lives? Is she married?'

'At the funeral, she told me she lives here in Verona. She was on her own then and at our wedding, but I don't know if she has a partner.'

'Any idea what she does for work?'

'I'm afraid I don't know. Rodolfo would have known, but he didn't talk about her very often.'

'Did you like her? Did your husband like her?'

Alessia nodded. 'Yes, I did, even though I hardly knew her, and I could see that Rodolfo liked her a lot, but at the wedding, every time he started to talk to her, he would see his mother glowering at him, so he would leave Tosca and scuttle back to his *mamma*. Needless to say, I didn't see Tosca go near her mother, either at the wedding or the funeral. Rodolfo and I had a brief conversation with her at the wedding but all too soon, Violetta dragged him away. I actually spoke more to Tosca at the funeral, when she appeared devastated at what had happened, but it was a matter of a very few minutes. In fact, now that I'm back here for a while, contacting her is near the top of my to-do list.'

At that moment, my phone started ringing. It was the inspector.

'Mr Armstrong, Ventura here. We've located her. You were right; she reverted to her father's name. She lives here in Verona and I'm planning on interviewing her tomorrow morning. You're very welcome to come along as well, if you like.'

This was excellent news. 'I would be delighted. Also, have you any plans to interview Alfredo Argento's wife, Ingrid? If so, and if it doesn't bother you, I'd be fascinated to sit in.'

'Certainly, I'll try and arrange both interviews tomorrow morning. Could you come down to the station at, say, nine o'clock? I'm not sure at this stage whether the suspects will come to us or we go to them.'

As I knew Anna was keen to carry on ferreting about in Verona's historic buildings the next day, I asked if he would mind if I brought Oscar with me. Ventura replied that he had no objection but then gave me the bad news. 'I've had the results back from the lab and none of the prints taken this afternoon match with the prints on the oil can. I'm afraid unless somebody new pops up – like the daughter, for example – we're back to zero on that one.'

The lack of a match came as no great surprise, but it was annoying all the same. I had been pinning my hopes on the can of brake fluid producing a breakthrough but maybe the appearance on the scene of Tosca would provide that for us.

When the call finished, I told Alessia about the oil can and our failure to find a match and received an unexpected explanation that should have occurred to me.

'Rodolfo changed the brake fluid in all his vehicles every three years. He did the same to my car only a few months ago – he said it was best practice. He was a perfectionist as far as his cars were concerned. I imagine *he* must have done it.'

I suppressed a few expletives. It looked as though there might be a perfectly innocent explanation for the oil can I had found, so did this mean that nobody had tampered with the brakes after all? Of course, there was still the unidentified set of prints on the can, but they could have been nothing more sinister than those of the salesperson who had sold the oil to Rodolfo. If so, could it be that the opera singer really had taken his own life after all? Was this investigation a waste of time? I snorted into the remains of my salmon salad but then reminded myself that it had at least given me the chance to tick off another fine historic city from my bucket list.

After dinner, I took Oscar and Elektra for a walk as much for my benefit as for theirs. My head was spinning, trying desperately to think of a reason why this man who had apparently had it all – money, fame, love, happiness – might have decided to drive his Jaguar head first into a tree. His wife, his mother and his agent had all confirmed that he had had no money problems, others claimed that since marrying, he had been satisfied and contented with his love life and, of course, the Christmas concert in front of kings and queens was the proof that his career had been flying high. If so, what on earth could have made him want to end it all?

Even though I lacked evidence of any kind, yet again, I found myself discounting the suicide hypothesis and remaining steadfastly convinced that it had been murder. Exactly why I came to this conclusion was hard to justify and in the end, all I could do was put it down to some sort of ex-copper's hunch. In fairness, I had followed enough of these in my time to know that more often than not, they had proved to be correct. Hopefully, the interview with Rodolfo's sister, Tosca, would produce some results because, otherwise, we appeared to be heading towards a dead end with a distinct lack of evidence.

That night, for a change, I walked down across the open field to the tennis courts and I made a discovery – or rather it was made for me by Oscar and Elektra. Just on the other side of the two tennis courts was a meticulously trimmed hedge, and it was only when I heard the splashes that I realised what lay behind it. Sure enough, when I rounded the corner, I discovered that the villa boasted a fine swimming pool, with underwater lighting providing enough illumination for me to make out the two dogs in the water, paddling around most happily.

I let them cool down for a while and then, after a bit of a struggle, I managed to lure them out of the pool and back into the field. I was watching Oscar as he rolled around on his back on the grass, growling happily to himself and wagging his tail so hard that his whole body wagged with it, when I suddenly realised that I was looking at Elektra, not Oscar. He was a few feet further away in the shadows but, in the twilight, the two black Labs had looked the same. This had been a case of mistaken identity.

Mistaken identity suddenly set a bell ringing in my head and my mind returned to the case. What if Rodolfo Argento hadn't been the target of the murderer after all? What if he'd been killed by mistake? Could the accident have been staged to kill somebody else?

And the most likely person to occupy that position had to be his wife.

I sat down on a dry patch of grass and watched the two dogs as they chased each other around excitedly, hopefully drying themselves out as they did so. Could it really be that the whole direction of the inquiry should be shifted? Beppe had told me that Alessia used to enjoy driving the Jaguar and that she had been just about the only person to do so apart from him. Maybe, knowing that her own car needed a new exhaust, the murderer had sabotaged the Jaguar in the hope of killing her, rather than her husband. I remembered that she had told me that she had been planning on using the Jaguar to drive down to Verona on the afternoon of the crash, and that her husband's decision to head for the lake and a walk to clear his head had been a last-minute thing. This of course immediately threw up a host of new questions, starting with why?

Not to mention, who?

I deliberately took my time over the rest of the walk so that the dogs could dry off as much as possible but, even so, they were both still emanating a powerful smell of wet Labrador when I got back to Dolores's apartment. She greeted me with a tolerant smile as she surveyed her damp dog.

'Don't worry, Dan, Labs are Labs. They love the water.' She glanced down at the two of them in the weak lights of the hallway. 'Certainly, it's hard to tell them apart, isn't it? I'd better make sure I get the right dog. You wouldn't want to end up with Elektra instead of Oscar, would you?'

Or Rodolfo instead of Alessia...

18

FRIDAY MORNING

I dropped Anna off at the end of the Castelvecchio Bridge and drove on to the police station, luckily finding a free parking space quite close by. I was shown up to the inspector's office where I found him, as before, almost submerged beneath a pile of paperwork. He gave me a welcoming smile as he stood up to shake my hand.

'We've spoken to Ingrid Argento – whose aggressive attitude makes Violetta Argento sound like a pussycat – and she flatly refuses to come here to the station, so I've arranged for us to go to see her and then we can carry on to Tosca Nyisztor's house afterwards. Anything new at the villa?'

'Maybe: I just had a thought last night. Could it be that Rodolfo Argento wasn't the target? Could he have been killed by mistake?'

The inspector slumped back into his chair and waved me into the seat across the desk from him as he explored this new hypothesis. 'So you're saying it could be the murderer wasn't aiming for him but for somebody else... presumably his wife?'

'She's the only logical target apart from him. The groundsman told me that she often drove the Jaguar – but she was just about the only one – and her own car was going to need fixing so maybe the murderer took a chance.' I went on to tell him how Rodolfo's decision to take the car down to the lake after lunch had been unexpected, and the fact that Alessia had been planning on using it at two-thirty for her hair appointment.

He nodded sagely.

'And that surely implies inside knowledge. Who else could have known that her car needed to be fixed and that she was going down to Verona that afternoon? It has to be somebody at the villa.'

'That's the conclusion I've come to. Of course, it might have been chance and, equally likely, I might be wrong, but it's a thought.'

'It certainly is. One thing's for sure: we're going to need to dig more deeply into her background to find out if she might have enemies. Thanks for passing that on. I have a feeling you might be right. We need to sit down and have a long talk to her. Shall we do that later this morning?'

'Definitely. Thanks for including me.'

He grinned. 'It seems to me it's as much your investigation as mine. All help gratefully received.' He picked up a couple of the numerous files from his desk and tucked them under his arm. 'Anyway, let's start with Ingrid Argento and see what she has to say for herself. *In bocca al lupo.*' This expression translates literally as 'into the wolf's mouth' and I couldn't help glancing down at Oscar. The inspector followed my eyes. 'By the way, if she says anything about your dog, I'll tell her he's a sniffer dog, but I won't tell her what it is he sniffs.'

'Food mainly – and other dogs' butts.'

With the blue light flashing, the police car cut through the morning traffic and we were soon away from the busy central part of town and climbing a series of narrow, winding lanes up the hillside above the city until we reached a high stone wall and a pair of massive wooden gates. The driver pressed the button by the intercom on the gatepost and, when asked what we wanted, just replied with a terse, '*Polizia.*' The gates swung open and we drove along a short gravel drive to an unexpectedly modern house, quite possibly designed by the same architects who had built the new Agri Argento offices. The walls of the long, low, white building appeared to be made principally of plate glass and I found myself wondering how hot it was going to be inside and how much privacy the occupants might enjoy. However practical it might or might not be, it was clearly a very expensive architectural statement. But then, Alfredo Argento was not short of the necessary money to make such a statement.

We left the driver in the car and walked across to the front door, which opened before we got there – no doubt because the maid had been watching us from inside one of the plate-glass windows ever since our arrival. Without a word and with a dubious glance at Oscar, the maid – clad in a formal black dress and white apron – led us along a corridor to a magnificent living room looking out over a stunning view of the city. Although the temperature was in the thirties outside, the air con was doing a good job in here and I almost felt cold – but not as cold as the reception awaiting us. Sitting in the middle of the room on an ultramodern white sofa was a woman I immediately recognised from her sister-in-law's description. Alessia had described Ingrid as very beautiful and she hadn't been exaggerating. With her long, blonde hair, blue eyes, and trim figure, I could well imagine how she could have had her pick of Verona's eligible bachelors before selecting Alfredo. Good-looking or not, this morning, the expression on her face was about as welcoming as a rabid dog with a headache. And talking of dogs...

'Why have you brought that animal into my house?' Her tone was glacial but the inspector was a match for her.

'The dog is part of our team. It's all right, he's well trained and he won't make a mess of your beautiful house.'

Ingrid Argento made no attempt to ask us to sit down so we stayed on our feet and Oscar, sensing the atmosphere in the room, sat down smartly at my side like a real police dog. I watched the woman's face carefully as Ventura began his questions.

'Your name is Ingrid Argento and you're married to Alfredo Argento?'

In reply, she just gave the slightest hint of a nod and the inspector continued.

'Please can you tell me how long you've been married?'

'It will be ten years next month, but I fail to see why this is of any importance to you.'

Ventura ignored her comment. 'Please can you describe your relationship with your brother-in-law, Rodolfo Argento?'

'He was all right.' Not exactly a gushing endorsement, but I had already got the message that getting information out of the beautiful Ingrid wasn't going to be easy.

'You got on well with him?'

'Yes, on the rare occasions when I saw him.'

'When you say "rare", are we talking once a week, once a month or less often?'

'Once or twice a year.'

He raised his eyebrows. 'Even though you were living barely ten kilometres from each other?' She gave no reply so he carried on. 'And what about his wife? Did you get on well with her?'

Her already sour expression became positively acid. 'I've always done my best to avoid meeting her, so I have no relationship with her to speak of. Now that Rodolfo has died and the funeral's out of the way, I fully intend never to see her or speak to her again.'

'Can you tell me why you don't like her?'

There was a brief pause before she answered. 'She was completely unsuited for him, and I'm sure that she was responsible for him deciding to take his own life.'

'Unsuited how?'

'She only married him for his money. That was clear to everybody. She was using him, that's all.'

I caught the inspector's eye and decided to take a chance. 'So, from your point of view, it would have been better if *she'd* been killed rather than her husband?'

Ingrid turned her head towards me and I could almost feel the antagonism in her stare. 'It would have been better if nobody had been killed, don't you think?' Her tone was thick with irony, but maybe I had caught a flash of something – surely not guilt?

The inspector took over the questioning again. 'I'm afraid I have to inform you that it's very likely that your brother-in-law didn't take his own life, nor that he was involved in an accident, but that he was deliberately murdered.'

Now it was his turn to be subjected to a withering stare. 'My husband told me last night that you believed that nonsense – and that's what it is. I have absolutely no doubt that Rodolfo killed himself to get away from that awful woman.' For a moment, I thought I saw a spark of animation in her eyes. 'Have you any proof to justify your ridiculous supposition?'

Ventura shook his head and a gleam of triumph appeared on Ingrid's face. 'Why are you wasting your time, Inspector, and, more importantly, why are you wasting mine?'

He ignored the question. 'Please can you confirm your movements on the day of his death? I'm asking everybody this.'

'What day was it? You'll have to remind me.'

She was doing her best to sound blasé and uninterested but I, at least, wasn't buying it. Given that she knew full well that there was a criminal investigation taking place, it was scarcely credible that she wouldn't have that date engraved in her memory. *The lady doth protest too much, methinks...?*

The inspector humoured her. 'Tuesday the twelfth of July.'

Ingrid made a show of looking for her phone and then scrolling through it before giving us her answer. 'At ten o'clock in the morning, I had my yoga class, at twelve, I met up with Alfredo for lunch at the golf club, and in the afternoon, I had intended going to meet friends in town but by that time, the news of the accident had come through and Alfredo and I went up to the villa to see if we could be of help.'

'And could you?'

She shook her head angrily. 'Of course not. Rodolfo was dead and that was that. It was a waste of time, but Alfredo insisted we should be there.' There certainly wasn't much of the milk of human kindness about this woman and I noted that Oscar didn't even try to go near her.

'Did you speak to his wife or his mother?'

'No, Rosina handled all that sort of thing.'

'I note that you believe it to have been suicide but, if it *had* been murder, can you think of anybody who would have wanted Rodolfo dead?'

She gave an indifferent shrug of the shoulders. 'How should I know? Like I told you, I didn't see much of him, but I can't think of anybody off the top of my head who would have wanted to kill him.' Her voice filled with sarcasm. 'Surely that's your job – but I can tell you now that you're wasting your time. There's no doubt about it: he took his own life because of that awful woman.'

Ventura and I were pleased when we were able to get away and I noticed that Oscar didn't waste any time either. We were shown out by the expressionless maid and we waited until we were back in the car before talking. The inspector swivelled around in his seat and looked back at me with my remarkably subdued Labrador sitting to attention alongside me.

'She's originally from Bolzano, so that's probably where the icy welcome comes from.'

The very northernmost province of Italy, Alto Adige, high in the Dolomites, is an autonomous region. The area was under the control of the Austrian empire for over a hundred years until the end of the First World War. Although it is now a part of Italy, the native language of much of the population is still German. This provenance no doubt accounted for Ingrid's name and her blonde hair and blue eyes, although not necessarily her acid temperament.

Ventura gave me an enquiring look. 'What did you think of the ice princess?'

'I think it's safe to say that she's confirmed what we've been told so far about her and Alessia: definitely no love lost there at all. As a performance, it wasn't bad, but I got the feeling her guard occasionally slipped. When you told her you had no evidence, I'm sure the expression that flitted across her face was one of satisfaction. Why should she be pleased that we've found no evidence? Certainly, she did her best to ram home her point that it was suicide and it was clear that she'd be only too happy if you were to drop the investigation. The question is why? Might she have had something to do with Rodolfo's death?'

The inspector nodded. 'My feelings entirely. She's certainly a tough character. Might she and her husband really have conspired to commit murder? Anything's possible. I'm sure that maid could tell a few stories, but I can hardly call her in at this stage without my superiors coming down on me like a ton of bricks.'

'It's fair to say that either Ingrid or her husband could have had the opportunity – getting hold of a key to the garage wouldn't have been too hard for them, especially if Alfredo occasionally drove the cars. They also had the motive of trying to get full control of the company, but do I really see either of them as murderers? I didn't get that impression of Alfredo although I could believe his wife capable of anything. It might just be worth checking her background to see if she studied mechanical engineering or if she has a hidden love of classic cars, but I wouldn't hold my breath.'

He nodded. 'Definitely. Well, let's go and see what the victim's sister has to say for herself.'

19

FRIDAY MORNING

Tosca's house was barely a ten-minute drive from the plate-glass palace we had just visited, but it couldn't have been more different. This down-at-heel residential area of Verona probably dating back to the sixties or seventies consisted of bland four- or five-storey apartment blocks on either side of a road lined with parked cars – needless to say with not a single Bugatti among them. The local council had obviously made an attempt at landscaping the area a long time ago but all that remained now were a few trees, most of them with motorbikes and scooters chained to them. I was pleased to see that the police driver stayed with the car. It was the kind of place where you might have come back to find your wheels missing.

Inside block number seventeen, the entrance hall was unexpectedly clean – a whole lot different from some of the tower blocks on my patch back in London in my early days on the force – but there was that same familiar smell of boiled cabbage in the air. I found myself wondering idly when the last time I had tasted cabbage here in Italy had been, but obviously somebody must like the stuff.

The other pleasant surprise was that the lift was working and, seeing as Tosca's apartment was on the top floor, I was glad about that. When the lift doors opened on the fifth floor, we found ourselves on a landing with four doors leading off it and I was pleasantly surprised yet again. In spite of its unprepossessing surroundings, up here wasn't dirty or sinister as I had feared, just a bit neglected. The inspector headed for apartment twenty-one and rapped on the door. There was the sound of footsteps on the other side and then the door opened to reveal a face that instantly struck me as familiar. I found myself looking at a much younger version of Violetta, but without the diamond earrings – in fact without any jewellery – and my old copper's eye instantly noted that she wasn't wearing a wedding ring.

'Signora Tosca Nyisztor?' He produced his warrant card and held it out towards her. 'I'm Inspector Ventura.'

As she studied the document, I studied her. Unlike her mother's silver hair, hers was an attractive sandy colour and it hung down around her shoulders. She was wearing jeans and a white top and there was a businesslike, but wary, air to her. Returning her attention to the inspector, she stepped back and invited us in. As she did so, Oscar wandered over to nuzzle her with his nose and her expression lightened. I decided to introduce the two of us.

'Good morning, Signora Nyisztor, this is Oscar and my name is Dan Armstrong. I'm a British private investigator working with the inspector, trying to ascertain exactly what happened to your brother.' Until I knew what she thought of her mother, I refrained from mentioning that I'd been engaged by Violetta. If the two were at daggers drawn, she might refuse to speak to me.

She gave a vague nod towards me, but she bent down to ruffle Oscar's ears and he immediately rubbed up against her. I made a mental note that he appeared to have given Tosca his seal of approval – normally a good sign.

After the fairly scruffy exterior, I wasn't sure what I'd been expecting, but in fact the apartment was smart, clean, and well furnished. No specially commissioned portraits of her brother or expensive marble fireplaces, but it looked a whole lot more comfortable than I had been fearing. We sat down around a modern dining table at one end of the living room and the inspector started on his questions.

'You are Tosca Nyisztor and you live here?' She nodded and he continued. 'How long have you lived here?'

'Since last October. I've rented this flat for a year.' Her voice was low, her accent well educated with just a hint of Tuscan – no doubt as a result of the first eighteen years of her life living with her mother at Montevolpone.

'Are you married?'

She shook her head.

'Do you have a partner?'

For a moment, I thought she might be going to refuse to answer but I was wrong. 'No, I live on my own.'

'Can you tell me your occupation, please?'

'Commercial Translator.' She glanced at me for a second or two. 'English and Italian.'

I felt I had to respond. 'Have you studied English?' I remembered her mother telling me that Tosca had left home at eighteen and there had been no mention of higher education. To my surprise, she nodded.

'I did a degree in English and Italian literature, followed by an MA in Translation, at the University of Surrey.'

'You lived in England?'

My surprise must have shown since she shot me a little smile and answered in perfect English. 'It's hard to study at a UK university without living there.'

University courses, particularly postgraduate courses, in

England are notoriously expensive these days and I wondered how she had managed to fund a minimum of four years as a student. Had her mother given her an allowance? But if she had, it clearly hadn't extended to housing. I filed that question away for now and listened as the inspector continued.

'You know why we're here, don't you? We're investigating the murder of your brother, Rodolfo. I was hoping you might be able to help us.'

The smile that had appeared on her face disappeared instantly, to be replaced by blank amazement. 'Did you say "murder"? You think Rodolfo was deliberately killed? I thought it was an accident.'

'New evidence has come to light, indicating that the brakes of his car may have been tampered with.' Ventura and I now knew this to be less likely than we had hoped, but I didn't blame him for mentioning it. 'We have no definite proof as yet, but I'm afraid that for now, we're treating his death as suspicious. Anything you can tell us about him or the family will be helpful.'

She was still looking stunned but she nodded. 'I'm happy to help, but I imagine you've heard that I left home eighteen years ago and I haven't been back since.'

I decided to answer this one. 'Your mother already told me that – admittedly reluctantly. Would you mind telling us a little bit more about what happened?' I caught her eye. 'We're not trying to pry into your private life, but this is a murder investigation and any information that relates to your brother might potentially be of interest to us. Could I ask why you felt you had to split from your family?'

She looked me straight in the eye as she answered. 'The split was from my *mother*. I never knew my father but I loved my brother. Unfortunately, when I decided that I had no choice but to go off and leave my mother, she took over my brother's life completely and kept him from me.'

'But you were both adults? If you were eighteen, he would have been in his twenties.'

'You've met my mother, haven't you? If so, you must know what sort of person she is. She's always been used to getting her own way. The relationship she had with Rodolfo was suffocating, and he never had the strength to react against it. Putting it simply, she told him I was bad news, and he just accepted what she said.'

Ventura and I exchanged glances. This was what we had already heard about the unhealthy relationship between mother and son, and now it was clear that this had been to the detriment of the daughter. He picked up the conversation. 'I understand that you were invited to his wedding last September, so you must have been in contact with him?'

'Only since the Christmas before last. Before that, I had had almost no contact at all – all thanks to my mother and her obsession with keeping him all to herself. I was living in London and I happened to see that he was performing at the Royal Opera House. On the news, they said that he was staying at the Savoy with one of his women – an American actress. It occurred to me that if the actress was with him then probably my mother wasn't so, on impulse, I dropped a letter into the hotel for him, not really expecting it to get to him and certainly not expecting a reply. To my surprise, the very next morning, I got a phone call from him and he took me out for lunch.'

'With his girlfriend?'

She shook her head. 'No, just the two of us, and no sign of my mother, I'm pleased to say. She was back in Tuscany. I spent all afternoon with him and it was wonderful. It was as if all the intervening years had disappeared and I'd got my big brother back, even if I felt sure it would only be until he returned to Italy and the clutches of my mother.'

'So you and he got on well together?'

She nodded emphatically. 'Like I said, it just seemed so natural. He talked to me about his career and I told him how I'd fled to England all those years ago, desperate to get away from my mother. I told him about my university course, about all the different jobs I'd done to try to make ends meet after my mother cut me off without a cent, and he told me he wanted to help me.'

'You mean financially?'

'Yes, even working all hours and selling what little jewellery I'd brought with me from Italy, I'd still racked up a massive debt and he told me he'd sort that out. Barely a week later, he sent me enough money to pay off all my debts in England plus, to my amazement, the news that he'd bought me a lovely little house here in Verona.' This time, when she looked up, there were tears in her eyes. 'I cried all that night. He told me he wanted his little sister near him again and you can't imagine how that made me feel after years of separation.'

'I thought you said this was a rented apartment?'

'This is just a temporary solution. The house Rodolfo gave me is four hundred years old and the builders have been working there for months – all pre-paid by my wonderful brother. They've promised me it'll be finished by the middle of next month and I can't wait to move in.' She ran the back of her hand over her eyes and the emotion in the room was palpable. If she was our murderer, she deserved an Oscar. Sensing the atmosphere, my very own Oscar got up and went around the table to sit alongside her, his head resting on her lap as he did his best to cheer her up.

She ruffled Oscar's ears with one hand while reaching for a tissue with the other. The inspector gave her a few moments before pressing on. 'Since coming back to Verona, did you see your brother regularly?'

She nodded. 'Every few weeks – he was away a lot for work and, of course, he'd just married Alessia. But it was so good to reestablish relations after so long.'

'Did your mother know that you and he were talking or that he was helping you financially?'

'He told her, and I'm surprised she didn't have a stroke. He told me she didn't like it one bit. Quite recently, maybe four or five months ago, she came up from Tuscany to see him and from what he told me afterwards, they had the biggest argument of his life. She ordered him to stop seeing me and he refused point-blank. Like I told you before, my mother can't stand not getting her own way, and according to him, she was incandescent.'

'But he carried on seeing you and helping you? After almost forty years of obeying his mother, what do you think made him finally stand up for himself?'

'I honestly don't know. Maybe seeing me as an adult and hearing how tough life had been for me while he'd always had everything. Maybe he felt guilty – although the fault lay with our mother.'

'And did you ever see your mother?'

'Apart from very briefly at the wedding and the funeral, no.'

'Did the two of you speak?'

'Not so much as a hello.'

'Can you think of anybody who might have wanted to harm him?'

'Absolutely not. Apart from being a lovely, sweet, immensely generous man, he was a national treasure.'

Ventura adopted an apologetic tone. 'I'm sorry I have to ask you this, but this is a murder investigation and that means asking some difficult questions. Could you tell me, please, whether your brother left you anything in his will?' From what Violetta had told me, I felt sure I already knew the answer and it came as no surprise to see Tosca shake her head.

'No, but I didn't expect anything. He'd been so amazingly generous to me already; how could I possibly expect him to leave me anything else?'

When we got back outside again, I glanced across at Ventura. 'That was either one of the most convincing performances I've ever seen in my life, or she really did love her brother.'

He nodded. 'I completely agree. I must admit that my opinion of her mother is going down by the hour. Can you believe she just cut her child off with nothing at the age of eighteen and, by the sound of it, didn't bother to make any effort to trace or contact her ever again? And then trying to tear the two siblings apart?' He ran his hand over his shaved head in disbelief. 'Whatever happened to motherly love?'

We stopped when we reached the police car – fortunately still with its wheels – and leant on the front wing in the sunlight while Oscar wandered over to leave his mark on a nearby tree. Ventura glanced across at me.

'So what have we got? Everybody loved the victim. He was a national treasure. Yes, he used to be a womaniser, but his new wife had sorted all that out. His bank records confirm that he was a very wealthy man who didn't owe anybody any money, no secret addictions, nothing. Why would anybody want to kill him?'

The same thoughts had been running through my head. 'The more I think about it, if it really was foul play – and I still believe that it was – who could possibly have had a motive to kill him?' I counted the possibles off on my fingers. 'His estranged sister who resented being sidelined by him but is now deeply grateful to him and has good reason to love him dearly. Two: his sister-in-law, with or without the help of her husband or his sister, who deliberately set out to murder first Rodolfo and now will have to murder his mother so as to inherit 100 per cent of the business. The problem with that is the fact that, according to the terms of his mother's new will, almost everything will in fact revert to Tosca after Violetta's death, so it would be pointless unless they kill the daughter too. Three murders? Do I see Alfredo, Rosina or Ingrid as serial killers? Honestly, no.'

The inspector nodded in agreement. 'But did they know that almost everything in Violetta's will is going to go to Tosca? She told me she only changed her will last week to that effect. One thing's for certain, I think we have to sit down and speak to Violetta and ensure that she spells out the terms of her new will to her nephew and niece at this afternoon's board meeting. That way, if they really are planning to make her their next victim, they should be made to realise how pointless it would be. What this new will does do, of course, is provide a motive for Tosca to now go ahead and kill the mother she hates.' He glanced at me and shook his head in disbelief. 'Maybe all that stuff about how much she loved her generous brother was just a fiction and she's the person who killed him and now she's preparing to kill her mother next so as to inherit what she sees as her birthright. God knows, I'm glad I'm not a multimillionaire. Money makes everything far too complicated.'

I added a few more possibilities. 'Another thought is that Ingrid and Rodolfo might have been having a clandestine affair and she murdered him in revenge after he dumped her to marry Alessia, but why wait almost a year to do it? And if it's none of the above, we also have Clarissa, the principal, who was allegedly dumped by Rodolfo when he met Alessia. Maybe she was so jealous, she decided to kill him off but, like Ingrid, why wait a year to do it? Alternatively, there might be somebody at the villa, like our would-be Casanova, Romeo, but it's tenuous in the extreme. And don't let's forget the theatrical agent who might have been desperate to inherit a million euros before Rodolfo changed his will, or the husband of the good-looking barista down by the lake, or some jealous lover from the past, and that's about all we've got.' I caught his eye. 'And this is assuming that Rodolfo was the murderer's intended target, and I'm still not convinced.'

Ventura nodded. 'Ever since you suggested that this morning, I've been thinking about what you said. If Alessia was the real target, then there's a very real risk that the killer might try again, hoping to do what he or she didn't manage to do the first time.' He raised his eyes to the heavens. 'Alessia might now be under threat, and the same could apply to her mother-in-law. I think you and I should head back to the villa now and sit down with both women and talk them through the possible ramifications of this case.'

'I'm not sure how Alessia's going to react, but I'm pretty certain that Violetta will blow a gasket when you suggest that she might be targeted by her own family. The problem, as we both know, is that we have no proof for the moment apart from a dodgy oil can. It's not a lot, is it?'

'Not a lot at all. Maybe I should just do as my boss keeps telling me and write Rodolfo's death off as an accident and leave it at that.' He looked across at me and said it before I did. 'The trouble is that I'm not built that way, and I can tell that you aren't either.'

20

FRIDAY LATE MORNING

We got to the villa at half past eleven and I was pleased to see Alessia's red Porsche parked outside. Hopefully, this meant that she was home. I spotted Dolores, who told me Violetta was in her apartment and had indicated that she would be lunching in the dining room before a car would come at two-thirty to ferry her to the Agri Argento head office for the board meeting at three. Safe in the knowledge that she wasn't going anywhere for now, we started with the grieving widow.

Alessia greeted us at the door of her apartment on the top floor and gave a special welcome to Oscar, who was clearly delighted to see her again. She led us into a huge living room and I took a good look around. The mantelpiece was far less cluttered than Violetta's and the only visible memento of her husband was an identical heart-shaped silver frame with his photo and the words *I love you*.

Alessia pointed at the French windows leading out onto the roof terrace.

'Why don't we sit outside? Make yourselves comfortable while I get us something to drink.'

At this time of the morning, the terrace was shaded from the sun and Ventura and I sat down in wicker armchairs, enjoying the gentle breeze. A few moments later, Alessia emerged with two bottles of cold beer and set them on the table before us. She had even brought a bowl of water for Oscar. I noticed that she opted for orange juice, which was probably a lot more sensible on a hot day, but, after the morning of questioning, a cold beer suited me just fine. The inspector thanked her for her hospitality and decided to get straight down to brass tacks.

'As you know, we're investigating your husband's death, and another theory has presented itself. Given that you also often drove the Jaguar, we have to consider the possibility that your husband was killed by mistake.'

She looked puzzled. 'I don't understand.'

'Could it be that the target wasn't your husband? What if the murderer was after you?' As he floated this idea across her, I watched her face closely, reading disbelief and then, understandably, fear.

'Somebody was trying to kill *me*?'

'As I say, it's a theory we're considering. I'm afraid this means I now have to ask you if you can think of anybody from your past who might have wished you harm: old boyfriends, professional rivals, anybody basically who disliked you a lot?'

I could imagine all too well the thoughts that must be rushing through her head. Assuming that she had had nothing to do with her husband's death – and I still considered this to be unlikely in spite of what Romeo had said – being informed that she might be at risk of being murdered must have been at best unsettling and more probably downright terrifying.

We had to wait almost a minute before she replied, shaking her head slowly from side to side as she tried to come to terms with what she'd just been told. Picking up that she was troubled, Oscar got up from my side and wandered over to rest his head against her leg in a gesture of canine support, just as he had done for Tosca. Anna had often said he had missed his vocation and should have been a therapy animal. Alessia looked down and fondled his ears as she attempted a reply.

'You really think that somebody might have been trying to murder *me* rather than Rodolfo? But why me? I can't think of anybody who might hate me to that extent. There are no skeletons in my cupboard that I'm aware of. I was married for three years when I was very young. That ended in divorce when I was twenty-four – that's thirteen years ago – but it wasn't an acrimonious divorce and he married again ages ago. We got married too young but were sensible enough to end things before they became unbearable. After that, I've had a number of boyfriends over the years but none were very serious and I can honestly say that none of those relationships ended particularly rancorously. As for professional rivals, yes, I'm sure there are some women out there who wish they were doing as well as I am, but I can't for a moment believe that any of them would actively consider trying to kill me.'

The inspector leant forward. 'Of course, another motive for murder can be money. Would you mind telling us if you have a will and, if so, what its terms are? What would happen if you were to die suddenly?'

A look of horror appeared on her face and he did his best to offer a little bit of encouragement. 'We're sorry we have to ask difficult questions and you don't need to worry about your safety. I'll make sure that nothing happens to you. What we're trying to work out is who could possibly have any motive to wish you harm.'

'I actually have an appointment with my lawyer next week to sort out my will. Now that I've inherited all this money, my accountant is very keen for me to get my affairs in order, but my head's been in such a spin over the past few weeks that I'm only just getting around to it now. After my divorce years ago, I'm pretty sure I altered my old will so as to leave everything to my parents – at least I think I did. I haven't seen it for years.'

I saw the inspector absorb this information. 'Would you be kind enough to contact your lawyer and ask him or her to check? Nothing sinister, I'm just trying to get hold of all the facts.'

Alessia was sounding very vague and it occurred to me that if she hadn't changed the old will, she might still leave everything to her former husband. And if this were the case, had we just found ourselves with another murder suspect?

Ventura returned to the possibility that she might be in danger. 'I think it's highly unlikely that your life is under threat, but for the next few days, at least until you've sorted out your new will, could I ask you to take special care? I would suggest that you stay here at the villa as much as possible and if you do have to go out, take somebody with you and make sure that your car is roadworthy before you do. I'm going to talk to my superiors when I get back to the office and, ideally, I'd like to station one or two of my officers here for a few days just to keep an eye on you and Signora Violetta.'

'Violetta? Might somebody be trying to kill her?' Alessia sounded bamboozled and I didn't blame her. I felt the same way myself.

'We really don't know but the inspector isn't taking any chances. Don't worry, it'll all be fine.'

As I spoke, Oscar turned his head towards me and I could read the scepticism in his eyes. I'm quite sure he sometimes under-stands far more than a dumb animal should.

At the end of our interview, just as I was heading for the door, Alessia added a postscript. 'They've told you about the concert tonight, haven't they? The academy's Midsummer Concert is an annual event, but this year, it promises to be very special in honour of Rodolfo. I'd be very pleased if you felt like coming along – that's you as well, Inspector, if you have time.'

Ventura looked pleased to be invited and we both accepted gracefully. Alessia then directed her attention at me. 'By the way, I phoned Tosca earlier and we had a long talk. I've invited her to the concert as well and she's going to come. Of course, this means she'll meet her mother this evening, but we'll worry about that when it happens.'

It was almost noon by the time we left Alessia's apartment and rang the bell to Violetta's flat in the corridor across the hallway. The door was opened almost immediately by a woman whose face I recognised from downstairs as one of the cleaning staff. She showed us through to the living room where Violetta greeted us cordially.

'Good morning, gentlemen, any developments?'

We all sat down and Ventura set out to explain as diplomatically as possible that it was just possible – not likely – that she might be in danger. Understandably, it took some time for the full implications of what he said to sink in.

'Let me see if I've got this right, Inspector. You think that Rodolfo was deliberately murdered so that I would inherit from him, and the murderer or murderers now intend to kill me as well. So what are you saying? As I told you yesterday, Mr Armstrong, in the event of my death I have little choice but to leave almost everything to my daughter, so are you saying you think Tosca killed her brother and now she's planning on killing me?' There was incredulity in her voice but also a cold edge to her words as though she maybe didn't see the allegations as so outrageous after all.

'We're not accusing anybody of anything for now, Signora Violetta, but it's something we're considering. The other possibility, as I'm sure you can appreciate, is that you might be in danger from your brother's children keen to take over complete control of the business.' As daylight dawned on Violetta's face, he continued. 'Just as they believed that they would inherit your son's share of the business when he died – only to be disappointed – it could be they believe it will finally come to them when *you* die.'

'Alfredo and Rosina?' She sounded stunned but, interestingly, quite a lot more surprised than at the possibility that her own daughter might be seeking to take her life. Quite clearly the rift between mother and daughter was far from healed. 'I can't believe for a moment that they would do anything so barbaric.' She looked across at both of us for a moment, her eyes steely. 'Ingrid, yes, I could believe anything of her, but I can't see how she could have operated without Alfredo, and I can't believe that he could possibly be involved in murder or, if you're right, multiple murders.'

I decided to take a chance. 'So if you can't see Alfredo and Rosina as murderers, what about Tosca? I know the two of you quarrelled all those years ago, but surely murder is excessive even in the most extreme of family feuds.'

She looked up at me and there was fire in her eyes. 'How should I know? I haven't seen her since she was a child. For all I know, she could have robbed a bank years ago and served a prison sentence by now. The little girl I knew was difficult, argumentative, and rebellious but she wasn't a murderer. What she's become now is anybody's guess.'

'So you really think your daughter might have killed her brother and might be planning to kill you?' The incredulity in the inspector's voice was plain to hear and it must have got through to Violetta as I saw her straighten up and breathe deeply.

'When you put it as bluntly as that, Inspector, it's unthinkable. My opinion of my daughter is based on my memory of a spoiled, attention-seeking teenager who had the nerve to insult me to my face and then go off and desert the family home. This doesn't make her a murderer and it's wrong of me to even consider such a possibility.'

I was genuinely surprised. Maybe beneath the cold, hard exterior, there might still be some relic of the maternal instinct. I came very close to asking her why she thought her daughter had taken the drastic step of leaving home eighteen years ago but I stayed silent. Now that she was sounding more reasonable, there was no point in stirring things up. Instead, I adopted a reassuring tone.

'We must stress that these are just ideas for now and you shouldn't begin to suspect your family. In a murder investigation, we have to consider all possibilities and these are just two. Something else that occurred to us quite recently was that maybe your son wasn't the killer's intended victim. Maybe the accident was arranged so as to eliminate Alessia – after all, she also drove the Jaguar. Do you have any thoughts on that hypothesis?'

When Violetta looked up from her hands, the old familiar fire was back in her eyes. 'I can well imagine somebody like her having made enemies. I dare say there are men and women in her past who hated her enough to want to kill her. I'll tell you straight – if the result of the accident had been her death, you wouldn't have found me shedding any tears.'

I hadn't been expecting sympathy, but the venom in her voice was chilling. For a moment, I once again found myself wondering whether this silver-haired lady might have engineered the whole thing, only to remember that it had been she who had got me involved with the case in the first place. Stifling a sensation of revulsion at such bitterness, I continued.

'Apart from men or women from her past or their partners, can you think of anybody closer to home who might have wanted to get rid of her? Anybody here at the villa, for example?'

'Here? You mean somebody on the staff? Surely not. I suppose anything's possible but I have no idea who that could have been. And as for the students, I can't believe any of them could do such a thing, but you could try asking Dolores or Clarissa. They have more contact with students than I do.'

The inspector picked up the conversation. 'If you have any ideas, here's my card. Please contact me at any time. A word of advice: you have a board meeting this afternoon and I would strongly advise you to take the opportunity to pass on the information to your nephew and niece that, in the event of something happening to you, you intend leaving everything to your daughter. I'd be grateful if you could do it as tactfully as possible and avoid mentioning that I might be suspicious of them. Could you do that, please?'

To my surprise, she smiled, but it wasn't a happy smile. 'Of course, I'll do that this afternoon. It's probably time I informed them of how I intend to dispose of my estate. I'm rather looking forward to seeing the expression on Alfredo's face when I break the news to him that he won't be getting anything.'

Ventura and I exchanged glances. There was definitely a dark side to this woman.

The inspector got to his feet and thanked her for her time, finishing with the words, 'As far as any possible risk to you is concerned, it's my intention to station one of my officers here for the next few days and nights so you can be sure of your safety.'

'Thank you, Inspector. By the way, have you been invited to the Midsummer Concert tonight? It's going to be in memory of Rodolfo and I'm sure you'll enjoy it. I've invited his agent, Paolo Ruggieri, and his wife as well. They were very close.'

To what extent Violetta was likely to enjoy the concert when she discovered that her long-lost daughter was going to be there remained to be seen.

21

FRIDAY LUNCHTIME

The next two names on our list of interviewees were Clarissa – to quiz her on the exact nature of her relationship with the victim – and Romeo, to ascertain if he and Rodolfo really had crossed swords over a woman a couple of years earlier and to discover the exact nature of the argument he had had with Rodolfo just before his death. We found Romeo in the bar and so we started with him. Ventura flashed his warrant card and the three of us went over to a table in one corner of the big room. As we sat down, I kept my eyes on Romeo's face. He was still wearing his trademark cocky smile and I wondered how long that would last once he discovered that he was being treated as a suspect in a murder inquiry. In fact, it lasted only a few seconds until the inspector produced a voice recorder, placed it on the table in front of us and switched it on.

'Can I have your full name, please?'

'Zanin, Romeo.'

Ventura asked for his age and address and then things got interesting. 'Are you a full-time student or do you have a job throughout the rest of the year?'

'I help my father and my uncle in the family business.'

'And that is?'

'We sell cars. The garage has the franchise for several different makes.'

'So presumably you also service and repair cars?'

'Not personally, I only work in the office but, yes, we offer a full service to our clients.'

For a second or two, I caught the inspector's eye. Romeo had suddenly catapulted himself way up our list of suspects. He had opportunity because he was here close to where the Jaguar had been kept, and it now seemed very likely that his background in the motor trade would mean that he also had the means to drain the brake fluid. All we needed now was a convincing motive and the inspector got straight onto that.

'How well did you know Rodolfo Argento?'

'Reasonably well. I've been coming to these summer courses for three years now, and he was often around. Of course, he was a major celebrity, so it was rare for him to speak to somebody like me.'

'I've been told that he did indeed speak to you just a few minutes before his death. I understand that there was an argument between the two of you. Would you be so kind as to fill me in on exactly what provoked the argument?'

This time, when Romeo looked up, it was with an expression of considerable concern. Presumably, he was starting to realise how serious his position potentially was. 'It was all because of something I said. I told his wife I liked the dress she was wearing and Rodolfo went ballistic.'

Ventura didn't give him any time to collect himself. 'The way it was reported to me, your comment was rather more about her body than her clothes. Tell me, did you leave the dining room before him or after him that day?'

There was now a look of panic on Romeo's face. 'Before, I think, but, look, it was just a bit of a squabble, nothing serious. I certainly had nothing to do with the accident.' A more pleading tone entered his voice. 'You have to believe me. I just said something stupid, he snapped at me, and I apologised. That's all. I promise you.'

'I've also heard that this wasn't the only little "squabble" between the two of you.' Ventura deliberately highlighted the word with his fingers. 'I believe there was another one two years ago and it concerned a female student here called Rosanna. Does that ring any bells?'

Sweat was beading on Romeo's brow now and he was looking furtively from side to side, desperately hoping somebody would come along to bail him out. I spotted his cousin, Veronica, standing by the bar, staring across at us, but neither she nor anybody else came to his aid. 'Two years is a long time but, yes, I remember Rosanna. I thought she was into me but I very soon found out that Rodolfo had turned on the charm and lured her away. At the time, I was angry and I said some stupid things, but that's long forgotten.'

The inspector picked up on his words. 'It seems that you make a habit of saying stupid things, Signor Zanin. I think it would be fair to say that you and the victim didn't get on very well. It's clear you disliked each other. What I need to ascertain now is just how deep your animosity towards him ran. I'm trying to catch a murderer, and, the way things are looking, the finger of suspicion is definitely pointing in your direction.'

'No, really, you're wrong.' He was actually wringing his hands in desperation. 'I could never do anything like that. You have to believe me.' I wondered if I did believe him. The inspector had managed to drag him sufficiently far from his normal smug self that I felt he might even be speaking the truth – but I wasn't going to let him off the hook yet. Ventura probably felt the same way because he moved the conversation on.

'If it wasn't you, Signor Zanin, can you think of anybody else here at the villa who might have wished to see Rodolfo Argento harmed?'

Romeo immediately shook his head and lapsed into silence but Ventura made no comment and let him stew until Romeo finally looked up at us again. 'You didn't hear this from me, right? There may be nothing to it, and I certainly can't imagine her as a killer, but the fact is that Clarissa and Rodolfo were carrying on for quite some time until Alessia came along.' For a moment, a touch of his former conceit showed through. 'I know a thing or two about women and it was plain to see that Clarissa was bitterly hurt and furious with him after he dumped her.'

'Then tell me, please, Signor Zanin, from the depths of your understanding of the female psyche, why she should have waited over a year to take her revenge.' The mockery in Ventura's voice banished the smug expression from Romeo's face.

'I don't know... Maybe Alessia was the murderer. What if Clarissa and Rodolfo had started up again? Alessia travels around quite a lot. Maybe Rodolfo went back to Clarissa while she was away. Alessia came back, found out, and took her revenge on her cheating husband.'

'Can you substantiate that claim? Any proof?'

Romeo shook his head. 'No, I can't prove it, but I wouldn't have put it past him to have been cheating and I don't know Alessia well enough to be able to say she's a killer. One thing's for sure: when it came to women, Rodolfo was quite unscrupulous.'

I had pretty much written Alessia off as a potential murderer but hearing this hypothesis voiced by a third party made me stop and think. Had I maybe been too quick to dismiss her from my list of suspects? Had her apparent grief all been an act? I tried a couple of questions of my own. 'You say you don't know Alessia very well but how about Clarissa? How well do you know her? She seems very young for the position she occupies.'

Romeo rolled his eyes. 'You've noticed that, have you? We all did. Like I told you, when she was first appointed, we knew she'd been hand-picked by Rodolfo and it was clear from the start that there was something going on between them.' He hesitated before adding reluctantly, 'To be fair, she's good at her job, but I think we all know how she got it in the first place.'

And that was all we could get out of him. By the time we finished the interview, I had mixed feelings. On the one hand, it was plain to see that there had been animosity between him and the victim, but whether this could have led to murder was hard to assess. Certainly, with his background in the motor trade, Romeo had to remain high up on our list of suspects. The inspector finally dismissed him and it was a far more chastened and a far less cocky Romeo who headed for the bar and a large glass of brandy.

At that moment, the gong sounded and Oscar jumped to his feet. He had by now worked out that this signalled food. Everybody started moving towards the dining room and a few seconds later, Clarissa appeared at the door. Ventura made a beeline for her and, as a result, the three of us were able to choose a suitably isolated table for our conversation over lunch. The inspector waited until the waiter had brought wine and water before making a start on the interview. After taking down her name – Clarissa Delbosco – and the fact that she, like Dolores, lived in an apartment here at the villa, he moved straight to the crunch.

'I've heard from a number of sources that you and Rodolfo Argento used to be in a relationship and I'd very much like to know more about it. When did it start, when did it finish and how serious was it? I apologise for asking you such personal questions, but the fact is that I'm investigating a murder and I need all the information I can get.'

Clarissa's expression, which had been affable and relaxed up till now, instantly changed, but even for somebody like me, having spent half of my life trying to analyse what people were really thinking, she was hard to read. Underneath a veneer of embarrassment and indignation was something more. I kept a close eye on her and as she replied, it struck me that her overriding emotion appeared to be anger – or, at least, irritation.

'I understand that you have to ask these questions, Inspector, but it doesn't make them any easier to answer. I'm no fool. When Rodolfo offered me the position of principal almost three years ago now, I had a good idea what was really going through his head. In those days, he had a reputation for treating women appallingly and I took the job with my eyes wide open. The fact of the matter is that I'm well qualified and experienced to do a job like this and I set out to show everybody that I'd been appointed on my merits as a professional. I'm confident that if you ask any of the staff or students here what they think of my competence, you'll get positive replies.' She looked up at both of us, her expression firm and serious, but distinctly miffed. 'I didn't get the job because I was having an affair with Rodolfo and, although I'm the first to accept that he propositioned me on numerous occasions back at the start of my tenure here, nothing ever happened between us and, once I'd made my position clear, he always behaved as a complete gentleman towards me from then on.'

She was sounding measured and convincing but Ventura piled on the pressure all the same. 'I'm afraid that contradicts what I've been told, particularly with regard to the months immediately before he met his future wife. I've heard you described as being heartbroken when he abandoned you. Is that incorrect?'

She even managed to produce a trace of a smile. 'People can

think what they like, and some people have amazing powers of imagination, but I defy anybody to produce proof that my relationship with Rodolfo was anything but professional – yes, friendly of course, but never more than that,'

Again, she sounded convincing and the inspector and I exchanged glances before I tried a different tack. 'Are you aware that Rodolfo had a sister?'

She nodded. 'Tosca – one of Puccini's greatest operas and what a wonderful name for an opera aficionada. To be honest, I only heard about her very recently: yesterday, to be precise. Alessia told me she intended inviting Tosca to tonight's concert, particularly as we intend it to be a celebration of the life of Rodolfo. Of course I look forward to meeting her. Why do you ask?'

'Tosca has been estranged from her mother and brother for some years and she only met up with him again very recently, the Christmas before last.' I thought it worth trying to provoke some emotion, maybe jealousy, to break through Clarissa's deadpan reaction to the questioning. 'That would have been when you and he were reportedly in a relationship, but you might be interested to know that when Tosca met him, he was staying at the Savoy hotel in London with an American actress. How does that make you feel?'

'I repeat what I've just told you: I was not having an affair with him and so, in consequence, whether or not he was with an American actress is of no interest to me at all.' Once again, she sounded as if she was speaking the truth.

At that moment, a waiter arrived with our starters. Today these consisted of slices of grilled polenta, some topped with chopped radicchio, some with salami and some with mushrooms. It all tasted as good as it looked but I noticed that Clarissa barely picked at hers – but being interviewed in connection with a murder can do that to people.

Refreshed by the food and a mouthful of wine, the inspector moved the interview along. 'Another line of enquiry we're following is that maybe the real target of the murderer wasn't Rodolfo, but his wife. Can you think of any reason anybody might have had to wish to harm her?'

The colour drained from Clarissa's face and she looked genuinely shocked. 'Alessia? Of course not. At least, not as far as I know. Maybe there was somebody in her past, before she got married, but why wait until now to get even?'

'How do you get on with her?'

'I don't see her that often, but she seems nice.' As I knew well, 'nice' can mean anything from lovely to questionable and I was unable to ascertain from her tone the exact degree of 'niceness' she intended. Ventura carried on regardless.

'A question that we're asking everybody is whether you can think of any enemies Rodolfo might have had?' Seeing her shake her head, he tried adding a suggestion. 'On a professional level, can you think of anybody who might have been bitterly jealous of him?'

She looked up from her plate. 'I'm sure there are jealous people out there, but I can't for a moment think of anybody who might have been bitter enough to consider murder. I don't want to tell you your job, Inspector, but are you absolutely sure that it was murder? It was a very old car, after all. I don't know if you've ever been in an E-type, but the bonnet is so long and the seats are so close to the ground that it's hard to see out. Maybe it was a momentary lack of attention or maybe there was a problem with the brakes.'

Of course, she had a point. My discovery of the can of brake fluid had led to nothing and quite possibly had a completely inno-cent explanation and, without that, there was no proof of interfer-ence. It was hard to know how to answer without indicating that it was little more than a hunch. The inspector seemed to be similarly afflicted as I noticed that he devoted himself to finishing his antipasti over the next couple of minutes and he didn't respond. It did occur to me, however, that from the way she was talking, it sounded as though she had been in an E-type Jaguar at least once in her life. There weren't many of them around so did this indicate that she had indeed had a relationship with the victim in spite of her protestations to the contrary? Alternatively, maybe I was making too much of this – he might just have given her a lift to the shops.

The interview degenerated into a simple conversation about subjects as banal as the weather, the food and, of course, tonight's concert. As I listened to Clarissa listing the performers and the pieces they would be singing – most of which meant nothing to me although I felt sure Anna would have recognised them – it occurred to me that the guests would almost certainly include Alfredo, Ingrid and Rosina. With Alessia, Violetta and Tosca also going to be present, that meant we would have the whole Argento family together in one room. I looked forward to observing the dynamic of the group, particularly the Violetta/Tosca relationship. Similarly, it would be interesting to see how Ingrid handled Alessia after all the negative things she had said about her.

In fact, thinking about it, I realised that Romeo, Clarissa and Paolo Ruggieri would also be there, so tonight would see all our suspects in the same place. Would one of them turn out to be the killer?

22

FRIDAY AFTERNOON

Lunch was as good as ever and the main course a local speciality: roast guinea fowl in a wine sauce, served with a fascinating mix of mashed pumpkin and mascarpone cheese mousse. It was a refined dish and I felt sure Anna would be sorry to have missed it. I texted her to see how she was getting on with her historic tour of Verona and she replied almost immediately, telling me she was sitting in a café having a hot dog – hardly on the same gastronomic level as my lunch but no doubt satisfying all the same.

At the end of the meal, we shook hands with Clarissa and she went off to supervise the final preparations for tonight's event. Ventura and I went out into the grounds with Oscar and, when we were sure that nobody was listening in, we discussed what had been a busy morning.

We both agreed that, of the main suspects, Ingrid headed the list in that, as well as possibly having two motives – gain or revenge – she had been far and away the most unpleasant of the four, but there's a big difference between being a pain and committing murder. In second place was Romeo with his open animosity towards the victim and his knowledge of cars, although he had put up a pretty convincing display of proclaiming his innocence. He was followed by Clarissa, although she had replied to our questions with apparent sincerity, particularly demonstrating what appeared to be considerable respect and liking for Rodolfo, even if her support for Alessia had been a bit less enthusiastic. Least likely was Tosca, who had struck us both as genuine even though she, of all people, had potentially more to gain from the death of first her brother and then her mother. This of course left us with the barista down by the lake, who seemed unlikely, or the theatrical agent keen to get his hands on his million euros, but Ventura told me that in the interview he had had with one of the inspector's team this morning the man had broken down in tears and sobbed at the loss of his 'dear, dear friend'.

I asked Ventura what he thought of Romeo's theory that Rodolfo might have gone back to Clarissa more recently. What if the liaison had been uncovered by his wife, who had exacted brutal retribution? From what I knew of Alessia so far, I didn't see this as credible, but I was keen to see what the inspector thought.

'Anything's possible. With the exception of Ingrid Argento, everybody we've interviewed has been cooperative and believable – at least to some extent. Alessia came across as telling the truth, having been deeply in love with her husband and still missing him a lot, but you and I have met a great many talented actors in our time, haven't we? Personally, I tend to trust her, but she stays on the list of suspects.'

'And are we sure that none of the students apart from Romeo are in the frame? I must confess that I've been unable to dig up a shred of evidence against any of them.'

He shrugged his shoulders. 'Your guess is as good as mine. Yes, there are some good-looking women who might or might not have been involved with Rodolfo, but my people who interviewed everybody didn't find anything suspicious. For now, all we can do is concentrate on the main suspects.'

His phone started ringing. It was a short call and when it ended, he gave me the news. 'That was Alessia. She tells me she's checked the terms of her existing will with her lawyer and everything does indeed go to her parents if she dies.' He shook his head slowly. 'Pity, I was about to get my people to investigate her ex-husband, but I think this puts him in the clear.'

He called his boss at the station and received confirmation that a pair of officers would be allocated the task of spending the next three nights at the villa, deliberately creating an overt police presence, just in case the murderer might be thinking of striking again. If that were the case, those most at risk were Violetta and Alessia so the officers would be instructed to pay special attention to the top floor where they lived, along with Anna and myself. Needless to say, no sooner had Ventura contacted his superior than he was instructed to return to the *questura* to give a full report of the situation so far. Tonight's concert was scheduled for six o'clock, to be followed by dinner, and we agreed to meet up again here at five forty-five.

After he had left, I carried on for a longer walk with Oscar, my mind still on the case, turning over in my head the possible suspects and their answers to our questions. I was still deep in thought when I emerged from the vines to see a now familiar face.

'Beppe, good afternoon, hot enough for you?' The mid-afternoon temperature had to be well into the thirties and both Oscar and I had been hugging any shade we could find.

He took off his flat cap and fanned himself with it. 'Too hot for working in the fields. I'm just on my way back to the villa for a drink. How's your investigation going, or aren't you allowed to tell me?'

I set off through the field alongside him, dodging from scrap of shade to scrap of shade with Oscar glued to my legs. As for my answer, I kept it vague. 'The inspector's got his eye on a number of possible suspects but nothing definite yet.'

'My money's on it being a woman. Sooner or later, Rodolfo's past was sure to catch up with him.'

I nodded. 'It's a possibility but why wait until now? Most people agree that since meeting Alessia, he turned over a new leaf and no longer got up to his old antics.' As Beppe probably knew as much about the goings-on here at the villa as anybody, I added a question. 'Before Alessia came along, was he involved with any of the women here?'

He stopped in the shade of a huge chestnut tree and wiped his throat and neck with a handkerchief. As he did so, he took a cautious look around. 'Well, there was Clarissa, but I imagine you already know that.'

'People keep telling me they were together, but Clarissa herself denies it most vehemently.'

He gave me a knowing wink. 'Well, she would, wouldn't she? After all, he was the one who dumped her, not the other way around.'

'So you're saying they were carrying on together before Alessia came along?'

'Definitely.' He stopped and corrected himself. 'Well, let's say probably. I often saw them together, and, the way she looked at him, I reckon she was sweet on him.'

'But you have no concrete proof?' He shook his head reluctantly and I continued. 'And what about his attitude towards her? Do you think he was in love with her?'

He snorted. 'Love? I don't think he knew the meaning of the word – at least as far as fidelity was concerned. When it came to women, Rodolfo was a beast.'

Remembering Romeo's allegations, I tried another tack. 'And

after he married Alessia, maybe more recently while she's been away touring, do you think he and Clarissa got together?'

He gave a helpless shrug. 'Who knows? That's the sort of man he was, although I must say, he and Alessia did look so very happy together.'

Needless to say, this did little to resolve any of the issues going around in my head.

When we got back to the villa, I was very tempted to go upstairs and stand under a cold shower but, instead, I just went to the bar for a cold drink and a bowl of water for Oscar before going out to the scalding-hot van and setting off to pick up Anna in Verona. I had told her I'd pick her up at three-thirty and I found her waiting for me at the end of the Castelvecchio Bridge as arranged. She was looking as hot as I felt – even though I had the air con in the van on full – and the first thing she suggested was an ice cream. On the way down the hill from the villa, I had noticed a café boasting handmade *Gelato Artigianale* so I headed back up there.

Fifteen minutes later, we were sitting under a pergola covered with intertwined rambling roses, looking out over the city of Verona below us. From up here, it was clear to see the way the river curved around in a loop creating excellent natural defence for what had been an important city in the history of Italy and which today is over twice as large as the historic part of Venice, and the same size as the whole area of Greater Venice, making it a major commercial hub as well as a magnetic tourist attraction. The plains of the Veneto stretched out beyond the city but soon disappeared into the heat haze. At least up here, there was a hint of a breeze that wafted the scent of roses along the terrace. It was a very beautiful and a very romantic place and my companions apparently felt the same way. Anna reached over and took hold of my right hand and gave it a squeeze. At the exact same time, a hairy head landed on my thigh and a pair of big, brown eyes looked up at me. I gave Anna a kiss but limited myself to scratching the bridge of Oscar's nose. He likes that.

We consulted the menu and both chose the same thing: mixed fruit and chocolate ice-cream sundaes. At the bottom of the menu, I spotted a treat for Oscar and I ordered a strawberry-flavoured *gelato per cani* for him. As they say in the adverts, he's worth it.

Over our refreshing ice creams – needless to say, Oscar's didn't last long – Anna told me about her day in Verona visiting four different museums and even more churches. It sounded exhausting but she had obviously found it very fulfilling. I told her names of a few of the operatic pieces I could remember that we were going to be hearing tonight at the concert and gave her the news that this would also see all of our main suspects for Rodolfo's murder brought together under one roof. She looked up from her ice cream.

'How's the investigation going? Any front runners among the suspects?'

I gave her a brief rundown of the state of play so far and was interested to see that she had little doubt that either Ingrid or Tosca must have been involved and, in consequence, she thoroughly approved of the inspector's decision to place an officer on the landing outside Violetta and Alessia's rooms just in case. I didn't want to bore her by talking shop any more than necessary so I just told her that hopefully by now, Violetta would have informed her niece and nephew that murdering her would be pointless as far as they were concerned – unless they then murdered Tosca as well. I told her that I tended to believe that Tosca was innocent and left it at that, but she didn't look convinced.

'It seems to me that she's the one with most to gain from

Violetta's death. Maybe she's just a good actress. Maybe getting the suspects all together tonight will lead to a breakthrough.'

I took a mouthful of peach and white chocolate ice cream and nodded. 'I sincerely hope so. Put it this way: unless something does happen tonight, I have a feeling Rodolfo Argento's death is going to end up being put down to an unfortunate accident and that'll be that.'

Back at the villa, there was an atmosphere of barely concealed panic as the staff and students made the final preparations for the concert. This was to take place in the ballroom. Anna and I had never been in there so we took a quick peek through the doors. The room was huge, almost twice the size of the dining room, and the high arched ceiling was covered with spectacular frescoes depicting pastoral scenes with nymphs and shepherds in various stages of undress. Rows of seats had been set up in front of a low stage, and there were tables along one wall forming a bar where waiters and waitresses were already preparing Champagne glasses. I recognised a few familiar faces including Giorgio – AKA Rigoletto – and Luther Green, manhandling a big table across the room. In the far corner, I spotted Romeo snuggled close up alongside a very pretty girl and reflected that this particular leopard didn't appear to have changed its spots.

We were just turning away when we almost bumped into Clarissa. She was looking pale and Anna gave her an enquiring look. 'Are you all right, Clarissa?'

She nodded and then immediately shook her head. 'It must be something I've eaten. I'm afraid I've just been sick and I feel awful. I just hope I manage to hold it together for the concert. I need to stand up and welcome the guests at the beginning and say a few words about Rodolfo. At least when I've done that, I'll be free to go back to my room and lie down. Fortunately, Giorgio has volunteered to be Master of Ceremonies and introduce the performers, and Signora Violetta will say a few words at the end.' She shook her head ruefully. 'It just had to be on Midsummer Concert day, didn't it?'

We made commiserating noises and headed for the lift. Upstairs, I was impressed to see a police constable sitting on a chair directly between the stairs and the lift. Nobody would be able to get to any of the apartments without being spotted. We told him our names and showed him our ID and he ticked us off on his clipboard. Hopefully, this would mean that nothing sinister was going to happen up here tonight. We walked down the corridor to the two guest suites and, on impulse, I walked past ours to the next door and tapped on it. There was no reply so I turned the handle and found it unlocked. Inside, I saw a carbon copy of our suite, complete with stylish furnishings and French windows to the roof terrace. The bed was untouched and it was clear that this second guest suite was not being used. I had half wondered whether maybe a member of the family might be staying over, but obviously this was not the case. The top floor would house only Alessia, Violetta and us.

When we got inside our room, Oscar headed for his water bowl and then his basket, slumping into it with a satisfied grunt. Anna headed straight for the shower and I picked up my iPad, determined to research the suspects more thoroughly but, like my dog, I soon felt my eyes closing. It had been a busy day.

23

FRIDAY EARLY EVENING

At five forty-five, we tiptoed out of the room, leaving Oscar happily dreaming of squirrels – and maybe Elektra – and we headed down the stairs. I found Inspector Ventura waiting in the entrance lobby and I went over to see if he had any news. He shook his head gloomily.

'My people have been checking our main suspects and so far, it looks as though they were all telling the truth. Tosca Nyisztor did indeed live in London until last autumn and her brother did buy her a very nice old house in Verona. Romeo Zanin's family own the Renault main dealership in Vicenza, and Clarissa Delbosco spent eight years at La Scala in Milan before coming here. Interestingly, Ingrid Schwartz, now Ingrid Argento, was cautioned for abusive and violent behaviour twelve years ago. Clearly, she has a violent streak.' He shrugged his shoulders. 'But that's not much to go on.'

He had just finished talking when the front door was opened by a member of the villa staff and Ingrid appeared, followed by Alfredo. She was looking predictably stunning in a cream robe while he was wearing an immaculately tailored evening suit. He mustered a cheerful smile as they swept past us, but all we got from her was haughty disdain. Keeping a discreet distance, we followed behind, heading into the ballroom, and found it packed. People were milling around in front of the stage enjoying background music provided by a string quartet.

Anna helped herself to a glass of fizz from a waiter while Ventura and I chose to drink orange juice. Whether anything significant would happen tonight or not, we both wanted to be ready for it. Once inside, we stopped, surveying the room. On the far side, beyond all the people, was the stage where I spotted Clarissa, now changed into a long, black gown but still looking zonked. Closer to us was the Argento family group, consisting of Rosina, Alfredo, Ingrid, Violetta and Alessia. Alessia was standing beside Rosina while the body language of the other two women towards the widow was decidedly strained. I saw Alfredo making a manful effort to engineer small talk but without much apparent success.

A few steps away from them, I spotted Paolo Ruggieri along with his secretary/wife – now dolled up to the nines. They were hovering about, clearly keen to be invited into the family group but not daring to approach.

'Good evening.'

I turned to see Tosca, now with her hair up and wearing a charming, deep-blue evening gown. She looked very smart, every bit an Argento.

She held out her hand to the inspector and to me and I introduced Anna to her. I could see that she was looking very nervous and I didn't blame her. Fortunately, Alessia was the first of the family group to spot her and she came hurrying across to greet her sister-in-law with a hug and kisses. Alessia then gave us a little wave and, gripping Tosca's arm firmly in both her hands, led her across the room towards the family group. When they got there, Rosina greeted her with kisses on the cheeks while Alfredo, urbane as ever, produced a smile and a token handshake. At first, it looked as though the other two women were going to ignore her completely, then I saw her mother lean, reluctantly, towards her – but making no move to touch her – and utter a few words to which her daughter replied. Ingrid merely deigned to give Tosca a nod of the head and then a waitress appeared with a tray of drinks and they all helped themselves, no doubt pleased to have a diversion activity.

I felt Anna grasp my arm. 'It looks as though people are taking their places. I think we'd better go and sit down while there are still free seats.'

Reluctantly, the inspector and I turned away from the stilted cameo on the other side of the room and found three seats for ourselves roughly halfway into the audience. The background music died away and everybody took the hint to sit down, the Argento family in the front row, their faces annoyingly now out of our sight. There was no sign of the agent and his secretary/wife, who were presumably lost somewhere in the crowd. Clarissa appeared on the stage and waited for silence to fall on the room. Although she looked very smart and very professional, her cheeks were chalky white and she looked drained. Presumably, her digestive problems had not improved.

'Ladies and gentlemen, welcome to the seventh annual Midsummer Concert given by students here at the Argento Opera Academy. Thank you all for coming. I'm particularly pleased to welcome members of the Argento family, without whom this inspiring project would never have happened.' There was a ripple of uncertain applause, which strengthened as others joined in. 'As you know, we all suffered a terrible loss last month. We lost our beloved Rodolfo and this evening's concert is dedicated to his memory.' The emotion in her voice was almost palpable. 'We miss him terribly. God bless him.' She stepped back and gave a little bow before turning hastily away as the tears in her eyes sparkled in the spotlights. I saw her leave the stage by steps at the far side and disappear towards the back of the room, presumably on her way back to her apartment to lie down.

Her place on stage was taken by the jovial figure of Giorgio, no longer wearing his Rigoletto costume, but now a smart dinner jacket and bow tie. 'Ladies and gentlemen, it's my great pleasure to present to you the performers who will be entertaining you this evening. Firstly, special thanks to our friends from the Verona string quartet, who will be providing accompaniment.' There was another ripple of applause. 'And now I'd like you to sit back and enjoy the talents of our students. I know you won't be disappointed. First up, we have our youngest student, at the tender age of nineteen, please welcome Barbara Braunschweig as she sings "Caro Nome", that immortal aria from Verdi's *Rigoletto*.'

As the young German stepped forward and began to sing, I did indeed sit back and enjoy the performance – although part of me still couldn't help thinking of the chaos Oscar could have caused if he had been here. Her voice was perfect, and even as a self-confessed opera virgin, I could tell that young Barbara had a glittering future ahead of her. I joined in the enthusiastic applause when the aria came to an end and found myself looking forward to the rest of the programme. The concert continued with a choral group, more individual singers, some men, some women, some baritones, some sopranos, and the echoing bass voice of Amadeo Gramsci, who had so impressed us on Verdi Wednesday. Finally, at the end of an hour that had passed remarkably quickly, three young tenors – among them none other than Romeo – performed their version of Puccini's 'Nessun Dorma' that even I recognised from the World Cup back in the nineties. When the concert finished, all the students crowded onto the stage and enjoyed encore after encore from the appreciative audience – me included. As my first taste of live opera, it had been impressive, and I had a feeling I might be hooked.

After all the applause had died down, Violetta slowly climbed the stairs to the stage and walked gingerly across to the middle, eschewing the use of her walking stick. She congratulated the performers and then launched into an emotional eulogy for her son that drew tears from many onlookers. In particular, I could see Alessia's shoulders shaking and I felt for her. At the end of the emotional tribute, there was spontaneous applause from all sides and I joined in, although by now, I knew full well that Rodolfo Argento had been far from the saintly figure depicted by his mother.

Once the stage had cleared, we in the audience gradually vacated our seats and the inspector and I did our best to keep the Argento family group under observation. A waiter brought drinks for them and they were joined by what were probably local notables. All of them except Alessia helped themselves to Champagne, and a cog that had been slowly and subliminally turning in my head suddenly clicked into place. Alessia wasn't drinking alcohol, but I had seen a photo of her wedding where she and her husband had been toasting each other with glasses of Champagne. What did this mean – simply an attempt to reduce her alcohol intake or something else? And the something else that stops most women drinking is pregnancy. Could it be that Alessia was expecting her dead husband's baby?

Leaving Anna chatting to her soprano friend, Valentina Russo, I grabbed Ventura's arm and hurried him out of the room into the near-empty corridor where I wasted no time before telling him what had just occurred to me. He listened intently and I saw him digest the possible implications of this. I'd had a few seconds more to think about things so I said it first.

'If we assume for a moment that the accident was arranged so as to kill Alessia, not her husband, the problem we've been facing so far is why a jealous woman would have waited almost a year after the marriage to take revenge. What if the murderer somehow discovered that Alessia was expecting Rodolfo's baby? Could it be that Rodolfo had kept some poor woman hanging on while she desperately waited for his marriage to fall apart, only for her to learn that not only was it not about to fail but, if anything, the arrival of a child would only cement the relationship all the more?'

Ventura nodded a couple of times and looked up at me. 'And one of our suspects here tonight fits that bill perfectly.' He turned to the young constable who had come down to listen to the concert while keeping a close eye on Alessia and Violetta. 'Get back upstairs to your post, Varese. Check that all doors up there are locked and don't let anybody past you unless they're on your list. Got that?'

The officer disappeared towards the stairs and I ducked back into the ballroom to tell Anna I had things to do. After whispering a few words into her ear, I was just heading for the door again when I almost bumped into Alessia on her way out. The tracks of the tears on her cheeks were plain to see and she looked emotionally spent. She gave me a weak smile.

'I'm afraid I need to go and sit down somewhere quiet for a bit. Rodolfo's death is still so raw, and tonight has really brought home to me that I've lost a wonderful man.'

I walked with her to the lift door and waited with her until it opened. 'The constable is on duty up there and he'll make sure nobody comes to bother you.'

She nodded gratefully and, as soon as she had disappeared

into the lift, I hurried back to the inspector and saw that he had been able to locate Dolores. Together, we headed for the apartment belonging to the principal and knocked on the door repeatedly but there was no answer. Dolores had her master key with her and she unlocked the door for us. It was a nicely furnished little flat but it was empty. We went through to the bedroom and saw the bed untouched. Clearly Clarissa hadn't come back here to sleep off her stomach problems – if, indeed, she had had any. As I turned back towards the bed, my eye was drawn to a little heart-shaped silver frame on the bedside table. It came as no surprise to see that it contained that same photo of Rodolfo and the words *I love you*. I wondered if he had bought a job lot of them.

Ventura had also spotted the photo and he made the logical deduction. 'Our killer's got to be Clarissa. She was still in love with Rodolfo and he almost certainly played her along. She managed to keep it together when he left her for Alessia and then married, and she hung on, desperately hoping that the marriage would fail, but when he told her the news that they were expecting a baby, she cracked. We need to find her as soon as possible but, first things first, we need to make sure that Alessia's safe. You take the lift, I'll take the stairs. See you up there.'

The lift seemed to take an age to return to the ground floor and by the time I emerged onto the top floor, the inspector was already knocking at Alessia's door. He looked across at me, an expression of acute concern on his face. 'No reply, but Varese tells me she went inside less than five minutes ago.'

The officer nodded. 'And I checked all the doors when I got here. They're all locked except for the spare bedroom at the end of the corridor there, but it's empty. By the way, your dog has been barking.'

To reinforce his words, I heard Oscar making his presence felt in the distance. Interestingly, this wasn't his usual forlorn 'why have you gone off and deserted me?' bark but his aggressive 'something's going on' bark. I realised that he was alerting me to something that had happened and I set off down the corridor, shouting to Ventura to follow me, until I got to our room. As I opened it, Oscar came bounding out and headed straight for the door of the spare bedroom. He pushed it with his nose and it swung open. I followed him inside and saw immediately that the French windows were gaping wide. They had definitely been closed when I had looked in before, so this would appear to be the way a potential double murderer had gained access to the roof terrace and, from there, the way would have been clear as far as Alessia's apartment. I had no doubt now that Clarissa's stomach upset had been an attempt to establish an alibi while she had come up here intent on rectifying the awful mistake she had made the previous month when she had killed the love of her life instead of the woman she saw as the impediment to her happiness.

The inspector and I squeezed between the terracotta urns and raced after Oscar along the terrace towards the windows of Alessia's apartment at full speed. These, too, were wide open and I suddenly saw a movement over to one side of the terrace. Part hidden behind a massive banana tree in a pot were two figures, instantly recognisable as Clarissa with an unresponsive Alessia in her arms. Illuminated by the setting sun, Clarissa was manoeuvring the inert body of Alessia onto the parapet over the main façade of the villa and it was clear that she was intending to throw her rival for Rodolfo's affections off the roof.

There was no time to debate whether Alessia was already dead or just incapacitated, so Ventura and I threw ourselves towards the two of them. I managed to catch hold of Alessia's ankle and hang onto it for grim death while the inspector caught hold of her arm. Together, we wrestled Alessia's body away from Clarissa but, even as we did so, the principal jumped athletically onto the low wall and balanced there, the rays of the setting sun framing her body with a ghostly pinkish glow. She turned once towards us and the anguish on her face was all too clear before she turned back. Before either of us could get to her, she stepped into the void. One moment she was there; the next she was gone.

24

FRIDAY EVENING

Ventura and I stood just inside the front door with Oscar pressed against my leg on one side of me and Anna clutching my arm on the other. We looked on as the body of Clarissa was zipped into a bag and transferred into an unmarked van belonging to the forensic team. I was buzzing with mixed emotions. On the one hand, I was pleased we had managed to solve the mystery of who had killed Rodolfo Argento and why but, at the same time, I wished I'd been able to figure it out earlier and prevent Clarissa's death and the assault on Alessia. I felt that same bleak sensation in the pit of my stomach that had dogged me throughout my whole career at the sight of senseless deaths.

So close to the city of Romeo and Juliet – real or imaginary – Shakespeare would probably have appreciated this love story that had ended in tragedy, but to me, it all seemed such a terrible waste. An unprincipled man had ruined the life of a woman who had loved him dearly, and the result had been two deaths and a heartbroken wife and mother. Great opera singer he might have been but, as far as women were concerned, Rodolfo Argento had had the moral fibre of a sewer rat.

At that moment, I heard the lift doors behind us open and I turned to see two paramedics and a doctor emerge with a trolley and on it, propped up against a couple of pillows, was Alessia. The left side of her head was covered in surgical dressings but her eyes were open and she even managed to raise a little smile and a wave of the hand when she saw us – or more probably, when she saw Oscar.

As the paramedics took her out to the ambulance, the doctor stopped alongside us to report to the inspector.

'She remembers very little of what happened. As far as we can tell, her assailant was waiting for her when she let herself into the apartment and struck her with one of the fire irons, rendering her unconscious. It was a nasty wound, but she will recover. It's lucky you got there when you did.'

The inspector thanked him and turned to me. 'I need to get back upstairs to tell the Forensics people they can get on with their job now that the casualty has been removed.' He nodded towards the dining room and he gave me a wink. 'It'll be dinner time soon. Save me a seat. *Ciao*.'

After he'd left, I looked at my two companions. Oscar was already on his feet, nose pointing towards the dining room, while Anna was looking shellshocked at the rapidity and violence of the events that had unfolded here. I led her through to the bar and stopped to take a look around. There were probably a couple of dozen people here, milling about aimlessly, trying to make sense of what had just happened. Among them were the remnants of the Argento family group and the theatrical agent and his wife, still hovering in the background. As Violetta made eye contact with me, she immediately beckoned and I glanced back at Anna.

'I need to go and talk to the family, but you don't need to come unless you want to.'

She grabbed my arm with her free hand. 'I'll come with you. I'm interested to see how they react to what's happened.'

She wasn't the only one. In particular, I was dying to see how Violetta was going to react now that she knew that Alessia, rather than being the culprit, had almost become Clarissa's second victim.

We went across the room and I found that it was a reduced family group. There was no sign of Alfredo and Ingrid, so there were just three of them now: Violetta, Rosina and Tosca, standing in silence. The first to speak was Violetta, stating the obvious.

'We're all in shock.' She was looking her age now, and the other two looked similarly affected.

Fortunately, Oscar broke the ice by wandering around, nuzzling the three women and even managing to bring a hint of a smile to Tosca's face. Fair play to Violetta, she then had the guts to admit her mistake. 'I feel terrible. I was so very wrong about Alessia and I need to make it up to her. Tell me, Mr Armstrong, why do you think Clarissa did what she did?'

'It's clear that she was involved with Rodolfo before he met Alessia. Even after the marriage, she never stopped loving him, hoping against hope that the marriage would fail and she could have him back.' What I didn't voice was my suspicion that he had probably still been carrying on with her after getting married. This wouldn't help Clarissa now and it would only hurt Alessia.

'But what prompted her to murder Rodolfo if she loved him?' Rosina sounded as puzzled as they all looked.

'It was a mistake. Her intention was to murder Alessia.' I saw comprehension begin to dawn on the faces around me. 'And, instead, she killed the love of her life.'

Tosca was the first to react. 'But why now? Rodolfo and Alessia married almost a year ago. Why wait so long to try to kill Alessia?'

'This is unconfirmed at this point.' I paused, wondering

whether to voice my suspicions before deciding to just go for it. 'I may be wrong, but it's my belief that what tipped Clarissa over the edge was when she discovered that Alessia was expecting Rodolfo's child.'

All three faces in front of me looked stunned. I saw Violetta's mouth open and close a couple of times as she searched for words, but Rosina was the first to react. 'Alessia's pregnant? Can that really be true?'

I nodded. 'Like I say, it still needs to be confirmed, but that's my supposition. When she gets to hospital, that'll soon be checked.'

Violetta finally managed to regain the power of speech. 'You're telling us that Alessia might be bearing my grandchild?' She sounded overawed, but the bewildered expression slowly softened. 'You think she might be expecting Rodolfo's child? That's amazing and, if it's true, it's the most wonderful news.' A more serious expression appeared on her face. 'Let's just hope that tonight's events don't cause complications.'

I did my best to offer reassurance. 'She's in good hands, I'm sure.'

Violetta tapped me on the arm. 'I do so need to see her. Do you think if I went to the hospital now, I'd be able to talk to her?'

'I really don't know, but when they took her out to the ambulance, her eyes were open and she gave a little wave, so it's probably worth a try. Would you like me to call you a taxi?'

To my further surprise, it was Tosca who spoke up. 'I'd like to see her as well. I've got my car outside. I'll give you a lift if you like, Mamma.'

Violetta transferred her attention to her daughter and there was a pause before a little smile appeared on her face. 'Thank you, my dear. That's very kind.'

Anna and I exchanged glances. 'Mamma' and 'my dear' were

unexpectedly affectionate. Might this represent a thawing in relations between mother and daughter after so long?

Violetta transferred her attention to me once more. 'Thank you, Signor Armstrong, for all your help and for saving the life of my daughter-in-law. I'll be forever in your debt.'

'I only helped the police. Inspector Ventura is a good detective.'

We shook hands and then Tosca came across and, to my surprise, gave me a hug. 'Thank you, Mr Armstrong. Thank you for everything.'

The two of them headed for the door and that just left Rosina. She gave me a beaming smile and held out her hand towards me. 'And sincere thanks from me as well. My brother asked me to say the same, but he and Ingrid had to get away.' She gave me a little wink. 'An event at the golf club, I believe.'

'You aren't staying for dinner?'

She shook her head. 'After everything that's happened, I've lost my appetite completely. No, I just need to go home, sit down and relax. Thank you again.' She shook hands with Anna, ruffled Oscar's ears and turned for the door.

A waiter came past with a tray and I had no hesitation in helping myself to two glasses of Champagne. I handed one to Anna and had just taken a big mouthful when Paolo Ruggieri approached.

'Good evening, Signor Armstrong. So it's true that Rodolfo was murdered and his poor wife nearly met the same fate tonight. Will she survive?'

I assured the two of them that the prognosis from the medics was positive and they went off, still looking shocked. He would have been even more shocked if I had told him that until very recently, his name had been near the top of our list of suspects.

A few seconds later, the gong sounded and Oscar set off

towards the dining room door at pace. The events of this evening certainly hadn't harmed his appetite.

There were a lot of free seats tonight and I wasn't surprised. Proximity of violent death can have a very sobering effect on people. Anna and I sat down at a table and a few minutes later, I had an unexpected visitor.

'Signor Armstrong...?'

I looked up to see Romeo, an expression of awe on his face. 'Is it true that Clarissa murdered Rodolfo?' I nodded and he continued, his tone still one of disbelief. 'And tonight, she almost killed Alessia?'

I nodded. 'I'm afraid so. We only just stopped her in time, but we weren't quick enough to stop her jumping from the roof.'

He looked far from the self-confident – or should that be over-confident? – young man I had first met. 'But... why? What would make her do something as crazy and barbaric as that?'

I looked back up at him and gave a little smile. 'Love, Romeo, that's what. The word clearly meant a different thing to Rodolfo than it did to Clarissa, and this tragic ending is every bit as much his fault as hers.' I held out my hand towards him. 'Go and enjoy your dinner, and good luck with your career. I was most impressed with your singing. Keep charming the ladies, but never let yourself follow Rodolfo's example.'

No sooner had Romeo disappeared off to a table containing three women than the inspector returned, clapping me on the shoulder before sitting down. 'I'm sorry, I haven't thanked you yet. Without your help and insight, I have a feeling Rodolfo Argento's murder might have ended up being dismissed as an accident.' He pulled up a chair and sat down. 'My people have been searching Clarissa Delbosco's apartment. They've been checking her laptop and they tell me her browsing history is very interesting: brake failure, brake lines and a Jaguar E-type owners' club chat page.'

Anna shook her head sadly. 'Poor woman. Rodolfo really did treat her awfully.'

I let the inspector answer. 'You're quite right, but there's still no excuse for what she did, even though he ruined her life.' Keen to raise the mood, he called across to a passing waitress. 'Could I have a look at the wine list? I owe my friends here a bottle of the best wine in the house.' There was a movement at his feet and Oscar's head appeared alongside him. 'And ask the chef if he has a nice bit of steak for our four-legged friend. He deserves it.'

EPILOGUE
SATURDAY NIGHT

'Well, what did you think of *La Traviata* at the Arena?'

Dolores appeared carrying a massive silver platter. On it were two huge lobsters, a mountain of prawns and crayfish, and these were surrounded by a luxurious mixed salad containing everything from slices of avocado to pieces of Gorgonzola, orange and walnuts. Earlier today, Violetta, when she had heard that Anna and I were going to the opera, had insisted on asking the chef at the villa to provide us with an after-show dinner, but neither of us had been expecting anything on this scale, particularly at almost ten o'clock at night.

Alongside Dolores was Elektra and I saw Oscar jump to his feet as they approached. Anna glanced down at him as he stood there wagging his tail.

'He's going to miss his girlfriend when we leave tomorrow, isn't he? I had the feeling there might be romance blooming.'

I didn't comment. As Dolores reached the table, I could clearly see that Oscar's attention was on the food, rather than Elektra. The way to a man's heart is through his stomach after all…

Anna was the first to reply to Dolores. 'This food looks amazing, Do, please, thank the kitchen staff so very much. I hope they didn't have to stay later specially for us. As for the opera, we both loved it, and there was a very touching tribute to Rodolfo Argento at the start. His mother would have been very proud.'

I nodded in agreement. 'I thoroughly enjoyed it and, I'll be quite honest, I know so little about opera that I wasn't sure how it would affect me, but it was amazing. When we arrived here on Wednesday, the first person we met was Giorgio, in full Rigoletto costume. He said something then that came back to me this evening while I was sitting in the Arena. He said that opera wasn't just singing, it was for all the senses, and he's absolutely right. Tonight, yes, I enjoyed the singing, but it was the setting in that wonderful Roman amphitheatre, the delightful scenery, and the costumes of all the people on the stage that really made it for me. Am I likely to play opera music when I'm driving down the autostrada in the car tomorrow? Maybe not, but I know that if I get the chance to go to another opera, I'll jump at it for the sheer spectacle. So, in answer to your question, it was a terrific evening and this meal is absolutely perfect. Please thank everybody in the kitchens.'

When she went off to pass on our thanks to the kitchen staff, I looked across at Anna and raised my glass. On Violetta's instructions, we had been provided with a very good French Champagne to accompany our lobsters. The lights in the villa dining room had been dimmed and we were the only people in the room. 'I must call your daughter and thank her for giving us the tickets and forcing me to do something new. We both know that I came here seriously wondering whether I was going to need ear plugs, but I need to tell her the experiment worked. A delightful evening in delightful company.' I clinked my glass against hers and took a sip, savouring the feel of the bubbles against my tongue before letting the Champagne run down my throat.

Anna smiled back at me.

'I'm so glad, and our visit to the Lago di Garda this afternoon was fun too, wasn't it?'

Right on cue, Oscar's face appeared at my side, not looking in the least bit penitent. Driven by his love of water, he had chosen to leap into the lake and swim about for a good ten minutes, resisting all attempts by me to call him back. As a result, when we had delivered him to Dolores to look after while we went to the opera, he had still been damp and smelly, but she hadn't batted an eyelid.

I gave him a hard stare and pointed my finger at him, but that did absolutely no good at all. He just wagged his tail and reached up to lick my hand. Still, I told myself, without his barking last night, Alessia might now be dead, so an occasional swim was probably fair enough.

A bit later on, at the end of what had been a monumental and memorable meal, we had two visitors. I looked up as I heard the door and was delighted to see Alessia, accompanied by Violetta, who was holding her arm. Alessia still had a dressing on the side of her head just above her ear but, otherwise, she looked pretty normal. What was immediately obvious was that both she and her mother-in-law were smiling broadly. I stood up to shake hands, but Alessia was having none of it. She put her arms around my neck, pulled my head down, and kissed me on both cheeks before leaning close to my ear and whispering, 'I don't know what to say to the person who saved my life. Thank you doesn't seem enough somehow.'

As she stepped back, I gave both of them an answering smile. 'I'm delighted to see you up and about, Alessia. How are you?'

Violetta answered for her. 'They're both fine.'

Anna picked up on her choice of vocabulary. 'When you say they're both...?'

Violetta, still beaming, nodded emphatically. 'Three months already, and mother and baby doing well.'

We added our congratulations to the mother-to-be and the future grandmother and I reflected that this would be one child who would want for nothing – apart, of course, from a father. But the cheerful news hadn't finished yet. Violetta caught hold of my arm and gave me a more serious look. 'I thought you might be interested to learn that I'm going out for lunch tomorrow with Tosca. We have a lot of catching-up to do.'

After the two of them had disappeared upstairs, I looked across at Anna. 'Maybe things haven't worked out so badly after all.'

She nodded. 'All you've got to do now is to avoid exploding.' In answer to my bemused expression, she pointed across to the kitchen door. Dolores was advancing towards us carrying a tray loaded with the two biggest ice cream sundaes I'd ever seen.

I pointed under the table to where Oscar was stretched out on the floor, full of breadsticks, prawns and odd bits of lobster.

'It's all right; we'll have help if we need it.'

Oscar looked up and I swear he winked.

ACKNOWLEDGEMENTS

Warmest thanks as ever to my wonderful editor, Emily Ruston, and all the team at the outstanding Boldwood Books – especially Sue Smith and Emily Reader who do a wonderful job of correcting my mistakes. A special thank you to Mariangela, my wife of almost fifty years, who bears an uncanny resemblance to Anna when it comes to opera (and I to the self-confessed opera virgin, Dan). Her encyclopaedic knowledge of all things operatic has been immensely helpful. Thanks also to Phil Mason (he of the black fingernails) for his technical expertise in classic cars. Finally, massive thanks as ever to the talented Simon Mattacks for managing to bring Dan and the others to life in his outstanding audio performances.

ABOUT THE AUTHOR

T. A. Williams is the author of The Armstrong and Oscar Cozy Mystery Series, cosy crime stories set in his beloved Italy, featuring the adventures of DCI Armstrong and his labrador Oscar. Trevor lives in Devon with his Italian wife.

Sign up to T. A. Williams' mailing list here for news, competitions and updates on future books.

Visit T. A. Williams' website: www.tawilliamsbooks.com

Follow T. A. Williams' on social media:

x.com/TAWilliamsBooks

facebook.com/TrevorWilliamsBooks

ALSO BY T. A. WILLIAMS

The Armstrong and Oscar Cozy Mystery Series

Murder in Tuscany

Murder in Chianti

Murder in Florence

Murder in Siena

Murder at the Matterhorn

Murder at the Leaning Tower

Murder on the Italian Riviera

Murder in Portofino

Murder in Verona

Poison
& Pens

POISON & PENS IS THE HOME OF
COZY MYSTERIES SO POUR YOURSELF
A CUP OF TEA & GET SLEUTHING!

DISCOVER PAGE-TURNING NOVELS FROM
YOUR FAVOURITE AUTHORS &
MEET NEW FRIENDS

JOIN OUR
FACEBOOK GROUP

BIT.LYPOISONANDPENSFB

SIGN UP TO OUR
NEWSLETTER

BIT.LY/POISONANDPENSNEWS

Boldw**oo**d

Boldwood Books is an award-winning fiction publishing company seeking out the best stories from around the world.

Find out more at www.boldwoodbooks.com

Join our reader community for brilliant books, competitions and offers!

Follow us
@BoldwoodBooks
@TheBoldBookClub

Sign up to our weekly
deals newsletter

https://bit.ly/BoldwoodBNewsletter

Printed in Great Britain
by Amazon